IT WAS IMPOSSIBLE FOR TIME TO GO BACKWARD.
But so many things that once seemed impossible had
turned out not to be. What if Nella got things wrong,
but now she had a chance to get them right?

ALSO BY TRICIA SPRINGSTUBB

Moonpenny Island
Mo Wren, Lost and Found
What Happened on Fox Street

TRICIA SPRINGSTUBB

EVERY SINGLE SECOND

ILLUSTRATIONS BY DIANA SUDYKA

BALZER + BRAY
An Imprint of HarperCollins*Publishers*

ACKNOWLEDGMENTS

Once a book ventures into the world, it belongs to readers, not me. Yet I can't let this one go without saying that my deepest hope is that it sparks questions, conversations, discoveries, and most of all, new and deep connections. My heartfelt thanks to Donna Bray, Viana Siniscalchi, and all the genius people at HarperCollins who believed in this challenging book. *Mille grazie* to my agent, Sarah Davies; to my wonderful readers, Mary Oluonye, Delia Springstubb, and Kris Ohlson; to Mary Grimm and Susan Grimm for everything, including Mario Lanza; and to Mary Norris for her support and especially her knowledge of Italian.

Balzer + Bray is an imprint of HarperCollins Publishers.

Every Single Second
Text copyright © 2016 by Tricia Springstubb
Illustrations copyright © 2016 by Diana Sudyka
All rights reserved. Printed in the United States of America.

Library of Congress Control Number: 2015958372
ISBN 978-0-06-236629-0

Typography by Dana Fritts
17 18 19 20 21   BVG   10 9 8 7 6 5 4 3 2 1
❖
First paperback edition, 2017

For my family near and far,
who have been there for me
time and time again

N

MANZINI
HOUSE

SOCIAL
CLUB

VALUE VARIETY

ST. AMPHIBALUS

D'LON ANDREWS
NEIGHBORHOOD

ANGELA'S

GARFIELD
SCHOOL

At first Nella doesn't recognize the sound. The wind, maybe? Except the trees behind the stone wall don't move. A flock of birds with heavy wings? Except the sky is empty. Ghosts? Except of course that's ridiculous. A girl who's lived her whole life across from a graveyard does not let herself believe in ghosts.

The July night is warm, but she shivers. Until a few days ago, Nella knew every sight and sound, smell and taste of her neighborhood. The steep hill and narrow houses, the cheesy music at Mama Gemma's, the supernatural perfume of fresh doughnuts, and the zing of lemon ice. She and Angela used to love— No. Don't think about Angela. Just don't.

She starts down the hill. Past the deserted bocce court. The silent social club. The boarded-up school. Emptiness all around. The sound grows louder. It's almost dark and she should go home, but the sound tugs her forward. The hill is so steep, the houses and shops have to dig in and hang on with all their might. When Nella was still little, maybe seven or eight, she saw pictures of a landslide. She freaked. She imagined her neighborhood suddenly swept away, tumbled and crushed and reduced to piles of bone and rubble. Anthony, Angela's big brother, reassured her. *No landslides in this part of the world,* he said, shaking his princely head. Smiling with those deep-set eyes. Personally guaranteeing nothing bad would ever, ever, do you hear me *ever*, happen to her or Angela.

Anthony!

The world tilts and goes blurry.

"You okay?" asks a soft voice at her elbow.

A stranger. A woman with long dreads and dark, anxious eyes. Nella has almost reached the street where it happened, and suddenly she's surrounded by other people, all intent on getting to the source of that sound. Looking into the woman's concerned face, Nella at last recognizes what that sound is. Voices. Voices singing.

"I'm all right," says Nella, and then, who knows why, she says thank you in Italian. *"Mille grazie."*

The woman hesitates, but the sound, the singing, is pulling her, too. She reaches up—Nella is taller than she is—and gives Nella's head a motherly pat. Then disappears around the corner.

Police cars block off the street. Cops lean against them, arms folded. Maybe they're here to protect people, but they scare Nella. There are news vans, men with cameras on their shoulders. She looks around, recognizing no one. A tornado snatched up every person she knows and spun them away. An earthquake gobbled them down. A landslide pulverized them.

She slips between the barricades. A sea of strangers overflows the narrow street, spilling onto the sidewalks and little front lawns. Where did all these people come from? What are they singing? It sounds like a hymn, but not one Nella knows. She searches for Angela's face, her bright shining hair. Crazy! Of course she's not here. This is the last place on earth she'd be.

There was blood on the sidewalk, her little brother said. They washed it away, but you can still see it.

Nella squeezes her eyes shut. She can't stop shivering.

Wrapping her arms around herself, she thinks, *This is where it happened.* Thinks, *How could it happen?*

The voices rise, growing richer and stronger, gaining power till they turn into a solid thing, pushing hard against the darkness, trying to push it back and make something happen.

Or undo something that already did.

SECRET SISTERS
then

T hey met on the very first day of school.

The night before, Nella Sabatini laid out her uniform, a plaid jumper and round-collared blouse. She had new pink sneakers with snow-white laces she still didn't know how to tie.

And she had a lunch box. Her father had given it to her, proving again that he loved her best. The lunch box was pink, with her name in sparkly letters. For days Nella had carried it everywhere. That night, it stood on the kitchen counter, waiting to go to kindergarten with her.

Back then, Nella only had one little brother. Salvatore.

But her mother was pregnant again, and Nella was sure it was a sister. (Little did she guess that in the coming years her mother would bring home nothing but one fat, squally boy after another.) That night, Mom's back hurt too much for her to bend over, so Nella stood up on her bed for her good-night kiss. The plan was to leave Salvatore with Nonni, their crabby great-grandmother who lived nearby, and for both parents to walk her to St. Amphibalus Elementary School. Even back in those days, having her parents all to herself was a rare event. Put that together with starting school, and no wonder Nella couldn't sleep. No wonder she had strange dreams of her mother moaning and her father pacing, no wonder she thought she was still asleep when she felt his hand on her shoulder, shaking her. Not gently.

"The baby," he said. "The new baby's coming."

Nella rubbed her eyes. Baby? Today wasn't the baby's day. It was hers. Hers hers hers. She jumped out of bed, hoping her mother would tap her forehead and say, *You're right! How could I forget? Get dressed, Bella. I'll fix you a special lunch.*

But her mother stood clutching the edge of the kitchen table, her lips drawn back in a way that stopped the words in Nella's throat.

Then it was all a crazy confused rush, with her father

yelling at her to get dressed, and Salvatore wailing, and a wild ride to Nonni's, where Salvatore wailed even louder because he was scared of the old lady, and somehow they were pulling up beside the school and Nella, shoes still untied, was getting out of the car. Alone. Both her parents looked stricken. Maybe they would change their minds.

"You'll be okay, kiddo." Her father pointed toward the grown-ups standing on the playground. "They'll help you. And—"

But then her mother gave a cry, and he hit the gas.

That was when Nella remembered her beautiful new lunch box. Still standing on the kitchen counter.

The school was next to the church. On the edge of the asphalt school yard stood a statue of St. Amphibalus. His hand was raised in blessing, but his eyes were blank. No eyeballs. This was kind of creepy, but who else did she have? She huddled close, setting her hand on his foot.

Please let me have a friend.

"Look," said a voice. Another pink shoe appeared beside hers. The laces were dazzling white and tied in neat double bows. "We're twins."

That wasn't true. Nella had short curly brown hair, and this girl had long yellow braids. Once Nella had sat behind her in church, and it was all she could do not to reach out and stroke those silky braids. Besides, her own shoelaces were undone and already a little dirty.

"Don't cry," said the girl.

"I'm not!"

"Are you in kindergarten too?"

"My shoes aren't tied and I don't know how."

The girl ran away, making Nella start to cry for real, but within moments she was back, dragging a tall boy. The two of them could have stepped out of a fairy tale. She would live in a cottage in the woods, with her father the woodcutter, but he would be a prince, the lonesome kind, looking for true love.

His name was Anthony.

"Tie my friend's shoe," the girl commanded, and Prince Anthony bowed.

He had the same pale hair, but thick and curly. Cinderella, that's who Nella was when he crouched at her feet. He tied her laces in double bows to match his sister's, then stood up tall and straight.

"You two stick together," he said.

"Roger that," his sister said.

A big brother. A brother who looked out for you. (Destined for a lifetime of needy-pest brothers, Nella would always remember that moment.)

The girl, whose name was Angela, had gone to day care. She knew about forming a line, zipping your lips, and raising your hand. By lunchtime, Nella was doing everything Angela did. They were twins after all.

As they went into the lunchroom, she noticed Angela didn't have a lunch box either. That was comforting, until the lunch lady handed Angela a tray of food. Nella held out her hands, hoping for one too, but the woman, whose hair was trapped in a spidery web, ignored her.

"You don't get free?" Angela asked.

"No, I guess." Tears pushed at the back of Nella's eyes. Why couldn't she get free too? She was suddenly so hungry. The room was so loud. The thought of her beautiful lunch box, home on the counter, made her miss her mother so much. Nella slumped forward, her head in her arms.

"Bella."

Out of nowhere, her father loomed over her. He hadn't shaved, and his hair stood on end. He looked familiar but strange, nearly a stranger, in this strange place. With a jolt Nella understood: *The world is much bigger than they told me.*

"Great news, kiddo. You have another brother."

Daddy wasn't big on smiles, but he beamed as if he'd delivered the best news ever.

"What a day, huh?" He ruffled her hair. "He's got a set of lungs on him. I swear he's louder than Salvatore."

Angela sat very still, like a girl trying to memorize

everything she saw and heard.

"Nonni will pick you up. Keep Sal out of trouble. Wow, kiddo. You've got two little brothers now. You're Super Sister, know that?"

He dropped a kiss on top of her head and was gone. Leaving her there, red-eyed and lunchless.

"Your mom had a baby," said Angela softly. "I wish my mom would have a baby."

"A stupid brother!" The words burst out fierce and ragged. "I already got one of those. I want a sister!"

Angela blinked. She broke her chocolate chip cookie in half and put it in her mouth. Nella's own mouth watered.

"Don't cry," Angela said.

"I'm not!"

Angela held out the other half of the cookie.

"I don't got a sister either." Angela leaned forward till their foreheads touched. "You and me," she whispered. "We can be secret sisters."

Nella's mouth filled with sweetness.

"Okay," she whispered back.

AN ANNOUNCEMENT
now

Their seventh-grade classroom swam with the smells of lilacs and B.O. Sister Rosa had made a May altar in a corner of the room, with a statue of the Virgin Mary and armloads of perfumed blossoms. That sweet scent would make you dizzy, if not polluted by the reek of boys yet to learn the word *deodorant*. It was just after recess, where the boys hurtled around the asphalt playground bouncing off each other—like nuclear fission, her best friend, Clem, said. The girls clustered near the statue of old, eyeball-less St. Amphibalus.

Except for Angela, who stayed in to help Sister Rosa.

The way Angela sat on her hands now, Nella knew she was trying not to bite her nails. Her blond braids streamed down her back. Once upon a time Nella was jealous of those braids, but now they annoyed her, like so much else about Angela. She had beautiful hair—why didn't she leave it loose, or at least go for a ponytail? You'd think those perfect braids held her together. You'd think if she undid them, she'd come unglued.

Nella wanted to tell Angela about the braids but was afraid it would sound mean. Even though Nella no longer wanted anything to do with Angela, she didn't want to be mean.

Nella stretched her legs, her mile-long, ostrichlike legs that refused to stay under her desk. They had that kinked-up feeling—what if she was growing again? She was already a freak of nature, towering over everyone in the class, including Sister. Across the room, Clem's spiky head bent over a graphic novel. Casually, nonchalantly, Nella let her glance wander to the Knee of Sam. Which was, as usual, jiggling like crazy. This afternoon that restless knee had a streak of dried dirt shaped precisely like a fish. Nella smiled. Her face grew warmer yet. Raising her eyes, she discovered Sam looking back at her. *Knee stalker.* He grinned.

"My children!" Sister's voice was honey and cream, the voice of a young woman, though who knew how many

world and to be shining credits to our beloved school."

Sister Rosa dropped her face into her hands. More girls started crying. Sam pounded his knee with his fist, obliterating the mud-fish. Clem tapped her pointy nose, looking thoughtful rather than upset. But when Nella looked at Angela, she saw a mirror of her own disbelief.

The principal raised her arms, palms up. The signal to stand.

"Boys and girls, this is a very difficult time for us all. We need to remember the verse from Proverbs: 'Trust in the Lord with all your heart, and lean not on your own understanding.' Now let us pray."

Nella barely survived the afternoon. How could this happen? The school always was and always would be. She could pinpoint the exact lunchroom table where she sat the day Dad came to tell her Kevin was born, and the very desk where she suddenly, magically, knew how to read. The corner of the playground where she, but not Angela, joined the Disaster Dolls Club. The spot beside St. A's statue where she stood, mesmerized, the first time she saw Clem.

Clem. Nella had to talk to her. But when at last the day ended, Clem's father, Dr. Patchett, waited in his car across the street.

"Zoinks!" said Clem. "I have sax."

"Say you're sick! You are sick, aren't you?" Nella grabbed

her friend's pointy elbow. (Clem was the definition of *pointy*.) "I can't believe it! I love this school!"

"You do?" Clem looked surprised. "All you ever do is complain about the hideous uniforms and the meaning-less—"

"Still! It's my school. How can they just decide to close it? And force me to go to some strange, alien place where I won't know anyone?"

Clem's surprise morphed into mild amusement. "You're forgetting that's what I did, like just last year."

"Oh. I guess so." It was true—changing schools was nothing new for Clem. Dr. Patchett tapped the car horn.

"The mother ship awaits." Clem started toward the car. "Call you after sax!"

"Did she say call you after sex?"

Nella wheeled around to find Sam right behind her. She bent her knees in a futile attempt not to tower over him. She could feel the idiotic blush spreading across her cheeks.

"So good-bye, old St. Amphibian." He pulled off his tie. "Where you going next year?"

"How am I supposed to know? We just found out!"

"My parents said this would happen. Enrollment's way down, and it costs too much to maintain a school as old as this."

Nella bit her lip. She hadn't even known about the bishop's study. Her parents never said a word. That was so typical! Her mother was the world's most impractical person and her father . . . well, Nella and he didn't do a lot of communicating anymore.

"I'm going to give Garfield a try." Sam rocked back on his heels. "Considering how far away St. Moloc's is, plus tuition's higher."

"Garfield?"

Nella was shocked. That school had the world's scariest reputation. It was at the bottom of the hill, in that neighborhood. Everyone said the place had metal detectors but they didn't work, and all the kids carried weapons. The bathrooms had no doors. Detention was in a rat-infested basement.

Garfield kids were mostly black.

Nella didn't know a single black person.

There were maybe three in all of St. Amphibalus. Not counting Mrs. Turner, who cleaned at night.

Not that this had anything to do with anything.

Her bent knees gave a painful creak.

"We've got to bust out of this cocoon sooner or later. Why not sooner?" Sam's voice was confident, but worry flickered in his eyes. His nut-brown eyes, with their fringe of impossibly thick lashes. What he said next made her heart skip. "You should go too. We could stick together."

Before Nella recovered her voice, an eel slithered in between them. No, wait. It was Victoria. Her mascara was running. (No makeup allowed at St. Amphibalus, but Victoria got away with things.)

"Oh my God!" She laid her head on Sam's shoulder. Two inches shorter, she was the perfect fit for him. "We're getting split up! Oh. My. God."

Kimmy and the rest of Victoria's flock huddled around crying. Mob psychology—Nella had heard of it. Sam shoulder-hugged Victoria. He'd be sorry later when he found the mascara smears on his shirt.

"You should go to Garfield," Sam told Victoria. "We should all stick together."

Nella straightened her knees and charged across the school yard. Her little brother Kevin chased her, but she shook him off. On the edge of the yard, in the shadow of the statue of St. Amphibalus, stood Angela.

"I can't believe it," she said softly.

Me neither, Nella almost said. *My head's spinning! My heart's breaking! How could they do this to us?*

But she didn't want to be like Angela. Weak, watery Angela.

"It's not like we have a choice," she said.

Her clumsy, ocean-liner feet started running and didn't

stop even when she was up the hill and through the tall iron gates of the cemetery. And she kept on running, though the stitch in her side was killing her. She didn't stop till she got to the statue of Jeptha A. Stone, 1830–1894, where she collapsed in a miserable heap.

What the Statue of Jeptha A. Stone Would Say if It Could

I know this child. Her father is my faithful caretaker. Once a year, that good man climbs a ladder and expunges bird excrement from my shoulders and pate.

I, Jeptha A. Stone, am no fan of avian creatures.

When yet small, this girl helped her father plant the spring flowers. *Help* is a generous word. She was a clumsy child. Her father is a patient man.

I have not seen her in years. Her legs resemble a baby giraffe's. Still clumsy, I fear.

I sincerely wish she would not cry.

I, Jeptha A. Stone, am no fan of tears.

As you might guess, given my place of residence, tears are impossible to avoid. Tears, wails, laments. This place makes humans leak.

Sitting atop my magnificent marble pedestal, I am buffeted by other things besides grief. In winter, brutal winds assail me. Snow piles atop my noble cranium, and occasionally, icicles drip from my handsome, aquiline nose.

In summer, the heat beats down. The birds . . . well. You know what birds do.

Yet we statues must maintain our dignity. It is our solemn duty to be stoic. Imperturbable.

Above all, silent.

LAND OF INNOCENCE
then

The new baby, Kevin, wasn't even walking yet the morning Mom poured her coffee down the drain. The next day Nella had to pack her own lunch, because her mother was too busy throwing up.

(What were they thinking, making all those babies? Or more to the point, not thinking? It would be years before Nella asked questions like that. In first grade she still dwelled in the Land of Innocence, where her family was as much a given as rain or trees or God.)

This was the year that the balloon she got at the Feast slipped from her hand and tangled high in a tree, and when Anthony climbed up to get it, he fell and hit the sidewalk.

Anthony got a scar from that fall. A small slash over his left eye. Nella loved that scar. She secretly pretended he'd been in a sword fight to save her. Afterward, they galloped away on a golden horse with a silver mane.

Nella planned to marry him someday. In Real Life.

Anthony let Angela hold his hand even when his friends were around. (Not that he had many friends.) Nella longed to hold his hand too. When she imagined her hand in his, something inside her turned over. A little engine began to hum.

In first grade they learned to tie their shoes, to read, to recite the Our Father and Hail Mary. Their teacher, Sister Rosa, was a jolly old woman with round red cheeks—Nella and Angela were sure that was how she got her name. Sister liked to crush the two of them together in a hug and say they were her PB and J. "I can't have one without the other!" she'd crow.

(If only you could store up happiness, Nella would think years later. Dig a happiness hole, or keep a happiness piggy bank, saving up for when you ran out.)

Anthony walked them home every day. As they tightrope walked the bocce court wall, he sat and drew. A castle, a tiger, Nella with no front teeth. Once they found the skeleton of a small bird and he drew that, every weightless bone. He was never in a hurry to get home.

"You're an angel," Mom told him. "You should be named Angelo!"

"I'm named after my father." Anthony squared his shoulders, like just the mention of Mr. DeMarco set him at attention. "I'm carrying on the family name. It's an honor and a responsibility."

Mom's eyes clouded as if he'd said something sad. Then she put her arms around him, though by now he was too old to hug.

(Years later, Clem, no fan of hugs, would tell Nella, *When it comes to hugging, your mom doesn't discriminate based on race, religion, sex, age, or national origin.*)

FLIP OF A COIN
now

The cemetery was home to flocks of angels, granite or marble, fierce and sword wielding or cherubic and adorable.

It was also an arboretum, so the trees had identifying labels, just like the dead people.

RED MAPLE   WHITE OAK   EUROPEAN BEECH

STONE   WADE   PIERCE

More than a hundred years ago, boatloads of Italian craftsmen had arrived to build the cemetery's massive stone wall, lay out the gardens and curving paths, carve the angels and monuments and soaring obelisks. Settling nearby, they re-created the villages they'd left behind. They built the church and the school. They planted grapevines and fig trees, danced at each other's weddings, and wept at each other's funerals. Nonni and her husband, PopPop, came some years later, but things hadn't changed much. Nonni loved to tell about the old days, stories sweet and quaint as folk tales.

PopPop had worked in the cemetery. So had his son. And now his son, Nella's father, was the head groundskeeper.

Leaning against Jeptha A. Stone's monument, she remembered helping her father plant the spring flowers. He'd lift the seedlings from their plastic pots, and she'd tuck them into the wide flower beds. It was like setting zoo animals free from their cages. Afterward they'd walk home together, her small hand in his rough one. When people teased her father about how closemouthed he was, Nella was confused. It seemed like she and he were always talking, though he hardly said a word.

It was terrible how fast things could change. One second to the next. Like God flipped a coin.

Only of course He didn't. He had a plan.

Now Nella wiped her eyes. Jeptha A. Stone threw his self-important shadow across the grass and down the slope. If statues could see, he'd have the place's best view. Compared to sorry old St. Amphibalus, Jeptha A. Stone had piercing eyes. His wide brow wrinkled in thought. His coat fell from his wide shoulders in soft folds. STONE was chiseled into the monument base. His name, of course, but it also seemed like a description. *This is how lifelike a block of cold stone can be.*

As Nella stood up, a small, yellow-flecked bird landed on Jeptha's big bald head. Bright-eyed, it sang a merry *tra la la*, like it had laid the world's most colossal egg. In spite of everything, Nella had to laugh. It almost looked like the high and mighty Mr. Stone shuddered.

That night she went to Clem's house. The Patchetts were what certain people in the neighborhood considered Invaders. Clem's parents were professors at the university at the top of the hill. Her father dealt in quasars and quantums. He was like Einstein, only with normal hair. Mrs. Patchett wrote award-winning poetry that Nella couldn't understand any more than she could her baby brother's babble. They lived in the old public school, now converted into hip, green-energy condos. Their place had creaky wood floors and tall windows that rattled. A faint, ghostly smell of chalk and wet wool mittens still swirled through the hallways. The Patchett Parents loved old stuff—old rugs, old books, old bikes with fat funny tires. This was a different kind of old stuff from Nonni's, though. No doilies here. No porcelain ladies balancing baskets of grapes on their heads.

Nella and Clem were in Clem's bedroom. Sitting on the floor, Nella looked around at posters of Wolverine, Magneto, and Dr. Who. There was a chart of the elements, and a picture of a colossal pearl caught in a volleyball net. The space-time continuum, Clem called it. It was hard for Nella to draw the line between real and sci-fi. She was never sure what percentage of her best friend's mind was anchored in reality.

"It's so freaking cool. A leap second. Like a leap year, only nano. They actually *add* a second. They *extend* time. They *manipulate* the clock!"

Witness: Clem was talking about time. Time, at a time like this.

"Who are *they*? Wait, never mind! Not now. Clem, we have to talk about next year."

Clem crossed the room and lifted the top off her hedgehog's house. Yes, there was also a hedgehog, Mr. Tiggywinkle, Mr. T for short. His face was adorable, but as for the rest of him? *Gentle* and *decisive*—those were the keywords in a hedgehog relationship. GAD. Mr. T's black button eyes blinked and his nose twitched. He and Clem had similar hairstyles, come to think of it.

"They want me to go to that magnet school. The math and science one."

This was not news. Her parents had wanted Clem to go there this year, but by the time Clem took the admission test, she and Nella had become good friends. And Clem, whose test scores were normally off the charts, had scored abysmally low. Mysteriously, wondrously low.

"But . . ." Nella swallowed. "You flunked the admission test."

"You're allowed to take it every year. And this year they're adding an extra test date, since all these schools are getting closed." Clem lowered her prickly pet back into his house. "You can take it too."

Nella stared at Clem's digital clock. The red numbers stayed the same, stayed the same. In this room, time had died.

"I'd never get in."

"Don't say that." Clem's face suddenly loomed two inches away. Upside down, hanging off the bed. "Anyway, even if I get in, I don't have to go. I get to choose."

How did you score parents like that? How did you win

the super jackpot in the parent lottery? These were the sort of useless questions Nella's brain produced. Clem's square black glasses dangled from her forehead. She smelled like grapefruit, a smell that was nice but also a little dangerous.

"They don't believe in coercion, except on things like doing drugs or riding my bike without a helmet. Even if I get accepted, it's still my choice."

Nella scrambled up and hung her head over the edge too. The ceiling became the floor. The desk waved its legs in the air. Her upside-down heart skittered in her chest.

"So," she said. "All is undecided."

"And if I was Time Ninja, I'd freeze it right"—Clem jabbed the air—"here."

"Huh?"

"When you choose one thing, you dis-choose a gazillion others. *Making* a choice isn't the powerful part. *Having* a choice is."

Choices—Nella was terrible at them. Not that she got much practice, considering her life.

"But," she said, "what do you think you'll do?"

"I don't know."

"Are you faking?"

"Death to fakers!"

"Slow, lingering, torturous death."

"Fart!" they yelled together.

30

FART. Fakers Are Really Tacky, one of their secret two-person societies.

Nella's head was a blood bomb. She did a backward somersault onto the floor, then poked Clem in the belly. Or where a belly would be if she wasn't built like a breadstick.

"Your head will explode," Nella said. "And don't think I'm going to clean up all those spattered brains."

Clem laughed and slithered to the floor. They polished off their papaya juice.

"One thing is decided," Clem said. "Sam Ferraro's in like with you."

"Oh right. And Sister Mary Anne has a secret love life. She met this guy on match.com. He likes red wine. And Latin, of course."

"Too bad he's so conceited."

"Sister's boyfriend?"

"Sam Ferraro!" Clem shouted.

Why was she making this up? Boy-girl stuff didn't even interest her.

"Everyone knows he likes Victoria and her thong-wearing you-know-what," said Nella.

"His brain was so addled, he couldn't stop staring at you."

"Staring like he saw a Komodo dragon."

"Komodo dragons are adorable!"

In the living room, Clem's parents sat side by side with their laptops. Her father wore a bow tie. Nella had never seen him without it. Probably he wore it to bed. Her mother had swept-back, raven-black hair with a white stripe on one side. Cool. They were the definition of cool.

Clem snuggled between them. Mrs. Patchett tilted her laptop so Clem could see.

"Okay, bye," said Nella.

They all waved. One two three.

"Remember to think about the Leap Second!" called Clem.

"Okay," promised Nella.

The what?

Sinatra Torture poured out Mama Gemma's open door. *I did it my way!* If Nella heard that song one more time, she might actually, literally die. In the evening air, the spice of Mama Gemma's pizza battled the sugar of Franny's doughnuts, both smells bathed in grease. Grease—she was in love with it. No wonder her chin was a pimple farm.

The chairs outside the smoke shop, where certain neighborhood men sat and chewed repulsive cigars, were empty now. Except for one. She slowed down when she saw who sat in it. Mr. DeMarco had thick arms matted with yellow hair. His neck was wide, his eyes small. Angela and Anthony's father had his back against the wall the way he always did, laser eyes on perpetual watch. Unmoving as Jeptha A. Stone. As a dead man.

Nella hadn't always been scared of him. But she was now. She had been for years. She drew a breath, commanded her clunky feet not to trip.

"Hello, Mr. DeMarco."

No answer. Safely past, Nella looked back. He hadn't moved. Had he even heard her? His eyes pierced the distance, fixing on a point invisible to everyone else.

A dark shiver raced through her. Imagine having him for your father. How was it fair that Angela got a parent like that, while Clem got the Patchetts? What was God thinking, playing favorites like that?

Sometimes Nella really wondered about God.

She turned down her own street. A lonesome chill snaked off Mr. DeMarco and slithered after her.

BECAUSE ANGELA DIDN'T TELL
then

Papa. That's what Angela called him. In second grade, her every sentence started with his name.

"Papa's home for good now. Papa's discharged. Papa's going to get a job and live with us all the time. Papa took Mama out to dinner and bought her a lobster. Papa bought me a pink jacket. Papa says Anthony needs to man up. Papa Papa Papa . . ."

Slowly, it changed to "He."

"He's supposed to go to the VA hospital but he won't. He can't sleep at night, only in the day. Yesterday at the gas station the smell made him sick. He started shaking and sweating. I felt so bad for him, Nella."

And then . . .

"He got freaked out by a ceiling fan. He punishes Anthony for no reason. He tells my mother she's stupid. He says he misses his army buddies. He says nothing here makes sense."

That didn't make sense to Nella.

They were about to make their First Communions. That morning before school, Angela told Nella her father had bought her the most beautiful dress in the world. It was just like a bride dress.

"Can I come see?" Nella was so jealous. Her Communion dress was a hand-me-down from a cousin.

"It's in a special bag and I'm not allowed to take it out."

Angela never disobeyed her father. Or the teachers. Or any adult at all. Suddenly, Nella couldn't stand her.

"You're always so good!"

"No I'm not!"

Nella stomped away.

Late that afternoon, Angela appeared at the kitchen door. The Communion dress was draped across her arms, like it had fainted. They snuck up the stairs to the bathroom, where Nella locked the door.

How did it happen? One second Nella was tugging open the special bag's zipper, the next the dress was sliding over her head. It twinkled, a dress made of stars. Nella was so much taller than Angela, the dress pinched her armpits and bit her middle, but Nella still wished it was hers. She scrambled up onto the edge of the bathtub so she could see herself in the mirror over the sink.

"Be careful," said Angela.

Nella swished from side to side, tried to do a spin, and toppled into the tub. She felt the fabric strain and rip like her own skin.

Angela stared down at her, horrified. "It's ruined!"

"Ssh!" Nella jumped up. "Ssh!"

"I knew I shouldn't do it!"

Nella wanted to say sorry, but the word stuck in her throat. Turning away, she saw their reflections in the bathroom mirror, and that made things even worse. She was so much taller than Angela! Taller and sturdier, like their bones were made from different materials, and instead of feeling sorry, Nella felt . . . what did she feel? She didn't know the word for it, not yet.

"Nella!" Mom rapped on the locked door. "What's going on in there?"

"Nothing!"

"Open the door!"

A baby (which one would it have been?) on her hip, Mom stared at them.

"It's not my fault!" cried Nella. "I didn't mean it!"

"I'm going to get killed!" Angela began blubbering like she'd never stop.

Mom shifted the baby—Bobby it was—on her hip. She grabbed tissues, wiped Angela's snot, fingered the rip. It was incredible, what Mom could do with one arm.

"It's just a seam. I can fix it."

Mom whisked the dress through her sewing machine, mending it good as new. Smoothing the skirt, puffing the sleeves, she zipped it safely back inside the bag.

"I wish you were my mother," Angela blurted.

Mom was the world's least critical person, but this made her frown. "Don't say that. Just think if your mother heard you say that."

Angela rubbed her chin against Bobby's fuzzy head. "She wouldn't care."

After Angela left, Mom said, "The poor thing was scared to death. What goes on in that house?"

Nella wasn't in trouble. Because Angela didn't tattle. She didn't say, *Nella made me do it!*

"You be nice to Angela," Mom said.

"I am! She's my best friend."

"Good. That girl needs a friend like you."

The morning of her First Communion, Nella's father didn't get out of bed. Dad never got sick, or if he did, he wouldn't admit it.

Mom gave orders not to bother him, but just before they left for church, Nella crept upstairs. Her mother had added a wide satin sash to her hand-me-down dress, and Nella had a white veil and shiny white shoes. Nonni, whose usual present was underwear, had given her a white purse with stitched-on pearls.

She stood in the bedroom doorway. Her father's face was turned to the wall.

"Daddy?"

Nella had seen her father look bad—when the babies kept him up all night, or Nonni was sick, or when he drank too much at the social club. But never this bad. His face was gray. He winced as if looking at her was painful.

"Daddy?" Maybe he was having a bad dream and couldn't wake up. She went up on her toes. "See my dress?"

She put her palm on his forehead, feeling for a fever like Mom did. A mistake. He shrank away, making a sound so terrible, Nella jumped back. Something bad was trapped inside him, and it was trying to escape.

"Daddy! What's the matter?"

"Sorry. I'm so sorry, kiddo." He caught her hand and kissed her fingers. "Say a prayer for me today."

Mr. DeMarco wasn't at the church either.

"He had a hard night," whispered Angela.

"My father too," Nella whispered back.

38

Yet another sister secret.

Mrs. DeMarco was there, her hair limp, her eyes rimmed with red. Nella's mother had all those boys to manage herself, so Anthony was the one who took their photos. Nella's favorite was her and Angela holding hands with Sister Rosa.

"My PB and J!" Sister crowed, her cheeks rosy, her face beaming. "My Tick and Tock!"

They posed in front of St. Amphibalus—two small girls in white dresses, alongside a white stone statue. By some trick of the light or camera, the statue almost looked like it was about to speak.

What the Statue of Jeptha A. Stone Would Say if It Could

Hark unto me, Jeptha A. Stone!

Contrary to appearances, statues are neither stone blind nor stone deaf.

We see and hear all.

Then how can it be, one might ask, that we cannot speak? I have spent over a century pondering this. At first I conjectured it was because mortals, frail creatures that they be, could not bear the shock of discovering that blocks of wood and stone have opinions.

As time went on—and a monument is rich in nothing if not time—I came to another conclusion. I now believe that speech is such a great, such a powerful gift, it has been reserved for those whose hearts yet beat.

And yet, how many mortals squander that supreme gift? As they say nowadays, don't get me started.

NONNI, CROSS TO BEAR
now

Everyone had a cross to bear, Sister Rosa said. Nella's was named Nonni.

It was Nella's job to spend a few afternoons a week with her great-grandmother. Today when she got there, she found Nonni dozing in the chair by the window, Dad's First Communion photo in her lap. The table beside her was a Sea of Dad, Nonni's only grandchild. Here he was in his altar boy outfit, here in his scarlet Confirmation robe. Now he was graduating high school, first in his class.

Then, a gap.

The next time you saw him, he looked different. Not

41

so much older, but more worn. You could see he'd been through something, and it had stamped him for life.

In this photo he was getting married, to a tall, willowy girl in a dress too big for her. Mom, who considered clothes a waste of money, even bought her wedding dress secondhand.

Dad had no memory of his parents. They'd drowned when he was still a baby. A lake undertow had swept his mother away from shore, and his father, who couldn't swim, desperately tried to save her. All Dad could remember was life with Nonni and PopPop, which Nella took as a warning: Do not trust your memory.

Now she cracked the front window, and music drifted in. Conservatory students rented the house across the street, and they practiced all hours of the day and night. An old woman who was a clone of Nonni used to own that house, but when she died it turned into a rental. This was the neighborhood trend—the oldsters dying off, students moving in. Nonni hadn't liked the old woman, but she really hated the students. She hunkered by this window for hours each day, watching the dangerous Invaders across the street. More than once, seeing nonwhite kids, she punched 911 and croaked, *Come catch the Gypsy thieves!*

A Cross to Bear.

Nella sank into one of Nonni's numerous itchy chairs.

On the table sat a cup of watery tea. Nonni reused tea bags. She saved foil and plastic bags. She got everything at discount, even her beloved candy, so she ate jelly beans in December, and chocolate rabbits in July.

The music swelled like a bud about to bloom, like the spring day had turned into a song, and as if in answer Nella's legs began to kink and crimp. *Please don't make me grow any taller*, she prayed. If this kept up, one morning she'd wake up and her head would brush the sky. Her shadow would cause an eclipse. . . .

"Why you come?"

Nella opened her eyes. "Good to see you too, Nonni."

"What you want?"

To go. Immediately. "I came to make sure you ate lunch."

Nonni hesitated. Lately, she was confused when she first woke up. "I ate!" she said at last.

"What did you have?"

Okay, this was cruel. Nonni could forget things from a few minutes, let alone hours, ago. Her eyes narrowed.

"No fish!" She pressed her index and middle fingers together and shook them at Nella. "My cousin Al, he choke to death on a bone."

"Nonni, you love fish."

"Is wrong!"

For Nonni, Nella's wrongness was only a matter of

degree. She was wrong, wronger, or wrongest. Nonni especially hated Nella asking so many questions. *Girls ask too many questions,* she said, *God no answer their prayers.*

Like God wanted girls to be dumb?

Across the street the flower-music burst into full bloom, and Nonni hummed along under her breath. She loved listening, Nella could tell, though she'd never admit it. Just then, a boy raced up on a bike. An extremely cute white boy, with enough hair for two or three heads. Sam Ferraro might look like that, when he was in college. He took the front steps two at a time.

"Where Angela?"

It was eons since Angela last came along to visit, but Nonni always asked. Angela was her ideal girl. Pretty. Quiet. Knew her place.

Nella jumped up and headed for the kitchen.

She found some soup in the fridge. It was Mom's minestrone, special made, low salt, for Nonni. Left to herself, she'd live on candy. She had it stashed all over the house. Once Nella had found some on the back porch, on the shelf with Nonni's arsenal of bug and weed killers. *I'm not sure how much longer this can go on,* Mom said. *What is that supposed to mean?* Dad replied.

Dad was the only human being Nonni never badmouthed. This could almost be a reason to love her.

When Nella carried the mug of soup back to the

living room, her great-grandmother was spellbound by the view across the street. On the porch, Hairy Boy was trying to hug a girl with an enormous case strapped to her back. Turtle Girl wore a fluttery, cocoa-colored scarf that matched her skin. She was so petite. She probably wore size five shoes. As Hairy Boy leaned in for a kiss, Nella heaved a huge sigh, startling Nonni, who threw out an arm and knocked the mug of soup clean out of Nella's hand.

"Look what you did!"

Bits of carrot, shreds of beef, stringy celery, and pulpy tomato. It was a minestrone massacre. Nonni peeled a noodle off her sleeve and popped it into her mouth.

And then she laughed. Big, that's how Nonni laughed.

"Che schifo!" she said, wheezing.

This meant something along the lines of *This is so gross!* Nonni kept laughing, in between stuffing linty vegetables into her mouth. Nella ran to get a sponge.

"Your mama's cooking, no taste." Nonni grabbed the sponge and scrubbed at her sweater. *"Nulla!"*

Nothing. Way too close to *Nella.*

Across the street, the boy rode off on his bike, hair flapping like a great, fuzzy sail. The girl strolled away in the opposite direction, scarf fluttering. Everything about those two said *Yes!*

"God, He forget your mama's taste buds."

Nonni was right. Mom was a terrible cook. She was all about quantity, not quality. Nonni reached behind her and pulled out a bag of Jolly Ranchers. She took a handful, then passed it to Nella.

"Mi ricordo," she said. *I remember.* Nella sat back, unwrapping a blue raspberry, knowing a story was coming.

Once, when Nonni was a small girl back in Italy, she and her brother, Carlo, woke up early and hungry. They were always hungry, Nonni said, smoothing the candy bag. Hungry all the time. It was too early to wake their *madre*, who worked so hard. So Nonni went to the ice box and got out the heavy jug of milk. Both hands, it took both hands to get it to the table. Carlo climbed up on a chair.

"Boys! They no can wait!" Nonni laughed. "Like your brothers, no?"

The milk had a thick, delicious layer of cream on top. Before Nonni could stop him, Carlo plunged his little fist into the pitcher, tipping it sideways. The milk poured out, gushing over the table and onto the floor. Like a waterfall. Like an act of God. Like fate.

"I no could move." Nonni hunched her shoulders. "I was . . . was . . . hippo?"

"Hypnotized?"

"Hypnotized."

Nonni cradled the bag of jewel-colored candy in her lap. Most of her stories ended with disaster—Nonni was big on death and destruction—but this one was somehow different. Nella pictured her, eyes wide, spellbound by the mess. She and her brother, like miniature gods, gazed down on the chaos they'd unleashed.

"It's a good story," she said.

Nonni nodded.

By now it was time for her talk shows. When Nella said Dad would stop in on his way home from work, Nonni waved impatiently, fixated on a woman who got her head run over by a mail truck but lived to tell.

Outside, the world was blushing, only green instead of pink. Nonni's fig tree was still wrapped in winter burlap, but the air thrummed with the promise of spring. Standing on the porch, Nella felt a pang. Nonni used to be young. She really did. For a moment just now, she was a girl and an old woman at the same time. Nella remembered a drinking cup she got once for Girl Scout camp. With a tiny twist it collapsed flat as a coin. Time could be like that.

What was that thing Clem was so excited about? A jump second?

A small bird flew by, wings flashing yellow in the light.

Across the street, something shimmered on the sidewalk. The girl's scarf—it must have slipped off her shoulders. When Nella picked it up, the warm scent of almonds filled the air. *Finders keepers,* she told herself. And though she should have learned her lesson about being greedy, and taking things that weren't hers, somehow she was stuffing the scarf into her pocket, making a getaway, praying nobody but that beady-eyed sidewalk pigeon saw.

What the Statue of
Jeptha A. Stone
Would Say if It Could

I was a man of substance and wealth. I dressed and ate well. My home was grandly appointed. Behold my monument, carved from the finest Italian marble by the finest craftsman. Notice how inferior the other monuments and statues are. Why, some of these poor saps even lack eyeballs!

I have been grandly memorialized, and with good reason. I was a man who commanded the utmost respect.

Hark unto me, Jeptha A. Stone! While I lived and breathed, I never would have tolerated a bird upon my pate.

Avaunt, I would have cried. *Begone! Shoo!*

Alas. My tongue is now stone.

And so I remain mute.

With a yellow bird singing merrily atop my head.

DISASTER DOLLS
then

Angela was always quiet, but in third grade she became a mouse.

That was the year they learned about lines. Number lines, assembly lines, time lines. In religion, they learned about the line between good and evil. According to their teacher, you couldn't miss it any more than you could the Great Wall of China.

That year drew its own invisible line. Girls started acting differently. Some girls. They told jokes Nella and Angela didn't understand. And they started getting stuff. Sparkly shoelaces. Glow-in-the-dark bracelets. Disaster

Dolls, like Hannah who survived a hurricane, and Tess who survived a tsunami. Each came in a shimmery plastic egg, with a little book. Nella had never cared much for dolls (why would she, with all those real babies in the house?), but when her classmates started bringing theirs to school, and showing them to each other at recess, she discovered she wanted one too.

"I'd get Fiona, the forest fire one," she told Angela as they walked home with Anthony.

"Roger that." Angela still talked to Nella, of course. Talked more than ever, as if saving up everything for her. "And the earthquake one. Ella. She comes with a little dog she rescued."

By then Anthony was in high school, but whenever he could, he'd walk them home. His voice had gotten deep, and he had a new, deep smell, like the ground after a spring rainstorm. When Angela told him about Disaster Dolls, he laughed.

"Don't let those girls tell you what to want. Don't let them brainwash you."

Too late. Nella's brain was already washed. Still, she knew better than to ask for a new toy when it wasn't her birthday or Christmas. The rule in her house was if one got a treat, they all had to. Any treat had to be times four (later, times five).

The situation was even more hopeless for Angela. Her father had reenlisted, but now he was back home. He'd gotten wounded, though you couldn't see where. He had medicine, Angela said. Zillions of pills. Her mother nagged him to take them, which made him yell at her. Once he started yelling, he couldn't stop. He yelled till he got hoarse. When Angela begged her mother not to make him mad, she told Angela to shut her stupid face.

This was a sister secret.

"He's worst to Anthony." They were pushing someone (who would it have been?) in the stroller. Bobby. It was Bobby, and Kevin was hanging on to its back like a suckerfish. Bobby thought it was a wonderful game to pull off his hat, fling it on the ground, and watch Angela pick it up. Again and again she tugged it back over his ears. "Last night he grabbed the pencil out of Anthony's hand and snapped it in two."

"What did Anthony do?"

Angela slid her eyes away. "Nothing."

That was somehow scarier than if they'd had a fight.

"Then last night." Angela chewed her braid.

"What? What happened?"

"I woke up and my father was sitting on my bed. Just sitting there all hunched over, like a cold wind was blowing on him. I asked him what was the matter, but he didn't answer. He was there but he wasn't."

Like a ghost, thought Nella. Though there were no such things.

Angela picked up Bobby's hat and stuck her hand inside. She made it talk like a puppet. "Sometimes I wish he'd go back in the army again!" said the hat. Angela immediately yanked it off. "No I don't! I take that back!"

Angela's father was a soldier, so that meant he was good and brave.

Angela's father scared his kids and made his wife cry, so that meant he was bad and cruel.

Just because you did one right thing, did it mean you were good?

And if that was true, did doing one wrong thing mean you were bad?

Third grade was when Nella started asking questions like that. At school, her teachers still knew all the answers. But at night, in bed, Nella got confused. It was like another girl had come to live inside her. All day this girl curled up and slept, but at night she sighed and woke up. She stood on her toes and stretched her arms. This girl was greedy. She wanted so many things. Forest Fire Fiona, but other things too. Some things, she didn't even know their names. That didn't stop this girl from wanting them. She stretched, she strained, she reached. It was like she wanted to leap free of gravity, leap clean off the ground!

Nella didn't tell anyone, not even Angela, about this.

(Later, Nella would wonder if that girl was to blame for her clumsiness. Clem said it was invisible gnomes that made her trip seventeen times a day. But maybe it was that other, restless girl who'd woken up inside her.)

The Disaster Doll owners formed a club. If you didn't have a doll, you weren't allowed. Nella told Angela this was against the law. It was a free country. Angela put the tip of her braid between her teeth, a habit that was starting to get on Nella's nerves.

One afternoon as Anthony walked them home, Angela suddenly began to cry.

"I asked Victoria to see her doll, and she said my family was so weird I'd contaminate it."

Anthony froze. His face became a thundercloud.

"And she said Nella . . ." Angela bit her lip.

"Me?" Nella stood still. A small shock zapped her, head to toe. "Did she bad-mouth my father?"

What in the world made her say that? Everyone liked Dad. At church or the store or the social club, they made jokes like "This guy? He's the last one to let you down!" and "Where he works? People are dying to get in!" Dad would pretend it was funny, like he hadn't heard it a million times.

Still. Sometimes a ripple went out around him. Sometimes she caught people flashing him second looks that made her uneasy. Every now and then, Mom hustled her past a conversation with a we-don't-do-gossip face.

(This was the year Nella realized their neighborhood was prime territory for a disastrous landslide. Anthony reassured her they were safe. If only he'd been right.)

"Those girls are the real natural disasters." Anthony rubbed the scar over his eye. He made his voice light, though his face was still dark with anger. "Who wants to go to Franny's?"

He paid for the doughnuts with quarters and dimes. He and Angela never had any money. So it was a surprise when, the next day after school, he told them he was headed down to Value Variety, and they could come if they wanted.

It was October. The day was warm but Anthony wore a bulky jacket. Valentine-red leaves drifted at their feet. In her head Nella repeated the names of the six daughters she and Anthony would have someday: Melissa, Miranda, Marybeth, Martina, Mia, and baby Molly.

"Wait out here," he said when they got to the store. "Do not come in no matter what."

This was the second surprise.

Nella and Angela stood close together, feeling nervous.

Back then, they were forbidden to come down here by themselves. When Nella's family drove through with Nonni, she made them roll up their windows and lock their doors while she clutched her purse tight in her lap. Danger lurked on every corner, according to Nonni, though to Nella, it looked a lot like her own neighborhood. Houses with peeling paint and rusty awnings. No doughnut shop, but the Chinese takeout place smelled good. No Frank Sinatra or Mario Lanza playing, but even back then, Nella was sick of those guys.

"I wish Anthony would hurry up," said Angela, shifting from foot to foot.

Nella tried to imagine living down here. She'd go to the public school, which everyone said was terrible, old and falling down (but wasn't St. Amphibalus old too?). Nella wondered if the girls who went there wanted Disaster Dolls too. Or did they want different things?

"What is he *doing* in there?" Angela whined.

Putting her face to the store window, Nella glimpsed Anthony. Carrying a loaf of bread, he disappeared down the toy aisle. Minutes later, the automatic door swung open and he came out with the bread in a plastic bag.

"Get moving," he ordered, not pausing.

He made them cross against the light, and took the hill so fast they couldn't keep up. He didn't slow down till they turned into the iron gates of the cemetery and scrambled up the grassy slope at the foot of Jeptha A. Stone's monument. Anthony was breathing hard. Nella's stomach was in knots. What was going on? He dropped the bag of bread and pulled something out from inside his jacket.

"Pick," he said, holding his hands behind his back.

Nella was always quicker than Angela. She tapped his left hand, and he held it out. There, in her beautiful shimmery egg, lay Forest Fire Fiona. In his right hand he had Vera, survivor of the volcano that had devastated her village.

"You got us these? For real?" Nella was in a fairy tale. Her wish had come true. By magic. By a handsome prince! The air around his head shimmered gold. "Thank you! Thank you, Anthony!"

Angela kept her own head down, not speaking.

"What are you waiting for?" Exasperated, Anthony pried the egg open and pushed the doll into his sister's hands. "Here! It's for you!"

Nella already had her doll out. How small Fiona was. It was funny how the other girls' dolls seemed bigger. But Nella danced her against the white marble base of the monument, already dreaming of tomorrow, when she and Angela could join the club. When that rotten Victoria would have to eat her words.

"I love my doll," Nella told Anthony. "I swear to love her into eternity." *Her and you.*

Carefully, Angela slipped her doll back inside its egg.

"I want to keep her clean," she said.

She was spoiling everything. Why wasn't she happy? Why didn't she say thank you? She was hurting her brother's feelings. Anthony's shoulders slumped, like he wished he'd never done it. Without a word, he started back toward the gate.

"Don't tell your parents," Angela told Nella.

Why? The word bloomed and faded on Nella's tongue. Something was wrong. You didn't have to understand what, exactly, to know it.

"This is a secret," Angela said. "A secret sister secret."

The next day, Angela didn't bring her doll to school.

"We don't get an allowance." She had her braid halfway

to her mouth but stopped herself. "If we get any money, Papa takes it and puts it in the bank."

"I already know that." Nella clutched Fiona. "What are you telling me that for?"

Angela didn't answer.

At recess, when Nella joined the other members of the Disaster Doll Club, Angela held back. Why was she so stubborn? *They* didn't snitch the dolls—Anthony did. It wasn't their fault! Besides, Anthony would never do anything bad, so it must be all right.

Angela made Nella so angry, Nella couldn't stand to look at her. Except she did. Peeking over her shoulder, she saw Angela huddled beside St. Amphibalus. Somehow his blank eyes looked sad and troubled. *Nella*. For a second, she imagined he whispered her name.

Her heart did a painful twist. A line drew itself down the middle of the school yard, and she wanted to be on both sides at once. When she turned back, all the dolls looked tiny, not just hers.

The next week, Victoria showed up wearing a sweater that buttoned down the back. And nobody cared about Disaster Dolls anymore.

AMONG THE BARBARIANS
now

Nella walked home, snitched scarf in her pocket. She waved to Mrs. Manzini, walking along with her toddler daughter. The little girl proudly carried a loaf of epi bread half as big as she was.

At Nella's house, the brothers lay in a TV coma. The only one who paid any attention to her was little Vinny. He lassoed her knees and she swooped him up. The boys had been born with eyes the color of blueberries, but they'd turned brown, all except for Vinny's. His were gray-blue, the color Nella thought the ocean must be.

"Promise you won't turn into a repulsive boy," she begged him.

Vinny replied in a language unknown to other humans. Babble babble. Gibber gibber. Two years old, and so far he couldn't talk. The doctor at the clinic said speech delay could be a symptom of serious problems. If Vinny didn't start making words soon, major intervention might be called for.

Vinny waved his hands. He arched his eyebrows. He didn't know he was on a deadline. Nella kissed his ear and set him back among the barbarians. She wandered into the kitchen, where every surface was crammed with industrial-size boxes of cereal, barrels of peanut butter, and baby wipes. Upstairs, the rooms were wall-to-wall beds. Once, Clem slept over for two nights before anyone even noticed.

Mom was chopping onions for sauce. Long hair swooped up in a clip, she wore a faded skirt and flip-flops that used to be Nella's. Mom was beautiful, but treated her beauty like a silly gift she never wanted. She was just out of high school when she married Dad and got straight to making babies, namely Nella.

"How's Nonni?" she asked.

"The same. Unfortunately."

"People only become more themselves as they age."

That was a depressing thought.

Mom smiled through her onion tears. She was an optimist. In the face of all contrary evidence, she considered Nella beautiful and brilliant. She was sure Nella would win a scholarship to a good Catholic high school, where she'd win a scholarship to an excellent college. Mom had it all planned out, which was amazing and also alarming, since Mom was a disaster at planning. Witness: four brothers and a house with one bathroom.

In the living room the troglodytes rolled around the floor making the lamps wobble. Mom called to them to stop, so they went on mute, wrestling in silence, which was pretty funny to watch. If you were a moron.

All at once they were on their feet, thundering toward the door. Dad radar. When Nella didn't move, her mother gave her a beseeching look.

"Go on." She wiped at her eyes. "Say hi to your father. He's had a long day."

Reluctantly, Nella stepped out on the porch. Farther uphill, the wall of the cemetery rose like the edge of a fortress. That wall was all a person saw from this porch, unless she tilted her head back and found the sky.

If there ever was a landslide, acres of graves would come down on their house. Buried by the buried.

Nella pulled the scarf out of her pocket. She twined its almond-scented softness round her neck as her father trudged toward them.

Dad always worked hard, but hardest of all in spring. The cemetery's trees needed trimming, the grass needed mowing, the flower beds needed planting and weeding. Almost three hundred acres, and he was in charge. He'd hardly be able to stay awake through dinner. The Neanderthals swarmed him.

"Dad! Dad! Dad!"

Dad swung the baby onto his shoulders and tucked wiggle-worm boys under his arms. He was the president of the USA, a rock star, and the quarterback who finally took the Browns to the Super Bowl, all in one—just ask the Sabatini brothers.

They didn't know what she knew.

"How's my Bella?" His voice turned soft for his only girl. But he didn't pause, just pulled the front door open, not expecting an answer.

BREAKDOWN
then

In fourth grade, they had weekly vocabulary words. *Yearn* was one of Nella's favorites. It made her think of birds at twilight, a princess gazing sadly out her window, a silver bell in the distance.

That year they learned another word, not on the vocabulary lists. In Nella's mind, this word appeared like a neon sign. **POPULAR**.

Popular. Suddenly, mysteriously, certain girls were. Life was once an art project covered with glitter, but that year some invisible giant picked it up and shook it till most of the glitter came loose and fell on the floor. What was left—the popular girls—stuck together in a hard, sparkly mass.

This was the year Mr. DeMarco tried to re-up, but the army wouldn't take him. On the surface, nothing changed. Angela came to school with her hair in the same neat braids, and Mr. DeMarco sat outside the smoke shop, chewing a cigar and spitting on the sidewalk. Sometimes he got a job pouring concrete or laying asphalt, but it never lasted more than a week or two.

One night when Angela slept over (she was still allowed to sleep over, though that would soon change), she told Nella that she didn't know where her mother was.

"She said she was going to stay with Aunt Ginny in Pittsburgh, but Anthony called, and Aunt Ginny said she's not there."

Nella sat up. Adults lied—she knew that much by now. But not mothers. "Maybe she got lost. Maybe something happened to her!"

Angela pulled her sleeping bag up to her chin. "She doesn't want my father to find her."

"What?"

"She . . ." Angela spoke to the ceiling. "Did you ever hear of a breakdown?"

Nella had, but with cars, not people.

"Anyway," Angela told the ceiling, "we don't know where she is."

Nella lay back down and held still, like their neighbor's dog did during thunderstorms. Like if he stayed perfectly motionless, the storm monster wouldn't notice him.

"Can't Anthony go find her?" she whispered.

"He won't. He hates her."

"Oh."

Angela's face was suddenly close. Too close.

"My father killed people."

Nella drew back.

"He was a soldier!" Angela said. "He had to."

It was true, Nella knew. But her brain spun. How did he do it? With a gun or a knife or a bomb? Did the people cry and plead for their lives, but he killed them anyway? "Thou shalt not kill" was the most obvious commandment, like did God even have to say it? Just stepping on a bug, feeling its body crush and flatten beneath your foot, felt wrong.

"It was a war," Angela said.

"I know," Nella whispered.

"He never, ever talks about it. But my mother told us. He saw his best buddy die. Papa was right there trying to save him but it was too late."

(Too late. Years later, Nella would decide these were life's cruelest words.)

"My mother said he saw kids die too."

Kids.

"She said he lost himself over there. She said she couldn't find him anymore."

Nella's hands were sweating, and a disgusting taste rose in the back of her mouth.

"But . . . ," she said. "But he wanted to go back into the army. He must like it, or else why would he go back?"

As soon as she said it, Nella knew it was the wrong question. Angela rolled over and wouldn't talk anymore. Nella scooched her sleeping bag away till no part of it touched Angela's.

Thank you, God. Thank you for my father, who would never hurt another human being. Thank you for my family that is normal and good and not like hers.

They were still secret sisters, but now Nella heard other girls whispering: Angela's braids were dumb. She smelled like cigars. Her parents were whack jobs. Nella didn't know what to do. She pretended not to hear.

Anthony did the shopping, cooking, and laundry, all the things Mrs. DeMarco once did, plus he got an after-school job. He had no time for friends or sports or other teenage stuff. If he managed to keep any money, he spent it on Angela—bracelets, hair clips, little glass animals. Sometimes he gave Nella a matching present, as if the two of them were best friends, same as ever.

They were, weren't they?

The older her brothers got, the more deeply they worshipped Angela. They never farted or burped in her presence, an act of extreme reverence. Angela would listen to endless explanations of who you had to destroy how in which video game. She pretended to guess their ridiculous riddles. She tickled Bobby and told Sal he was handsome—Sal, who had enormous ears and front teeth coming in at bizarre angles. Kevin said he wished she was his sister instead of Nella.

"Me too," said Nella.

Clearly, God had gotten mixed up when assigning brothers.

Nella and Angela took lunch to Nonni every Saturday, but that winter day Nella told Angela she'd go by herself. She could've explained that Nonni and her friend Ernestina had an appointment at Elena's Beauty Shop, but she didn't. Angela just said okay. In that quiet, annoying way of hers.

Nella walked up the hill to her great-grandmother's door, so technically she wasn't lying. She brushed snow off the mummified fig tree. And then she just stood there, not knowing what to do next. The old lady across the street stepped outside to throw bread for the birds. She waved at Nella.

"Freddo! Freddo!" she called, *Cold! Cold!* Then hurried back inside.

It was strange. When you were little, you never thought about what to do next. Your life just kept happening. But by the time you were ten, life grew these pauses. These spaces, when you looked around. Unsure.

The pigeons battled over the bread like it was the last food left on earth. Nella's breath made dragon puffs. She walked to the corner.

"Nella! Hey, Nella!"

Victoria. She was with Kimmy, another girl from their class, and a girl Nella had never met.

"This is my cousin Megan from Akron." Victoria sounded as awed as if introducing a supermodel. Megan was older. She wore eyeliner and big hoop earrings. "We're hanging out," said Victoria. "Want to come?"

Nella was so surprised, she barely got out an okay. They went to Franny's, and thank goodness she had just enough money so she could get a twist and cocoa, too. They stood outside Adele's Boutique while Megan criticized the clothes in the window. Megan had an iPod and let them take turns listening. Victoria sang along and did a little dance, and when Megan smiled, you'd think

Victoria had won first place on *Who's Got Talent?*

They walked up the hill, giggling as they slipped on the ice, and even though Nella didn't say much, and wished she'd worn her mittens, she started enjoying herself. Megan and Victoria walked together, and Nella walked beside Kimmy, who gave her a piece of gum and told Nella she liked her scarf. Nella said her mother knitted it, and Kimmy said her mother was so pretty and Nella looked a lot like her.

Just when things were going so well, Megan stopped in the middle of the sidewalk.

"I am so cold. This is so boring."

Victoria's face fell. For a second, Nella felt sorry for her. But then anger took over. Who died and made Megan Empress of the World?

"Wait," said Victoria, and Nella hoped she'd tell Megan to quit being so snotty. "I've got something to show you. You will not be bored, promise."

Megan yawned. Victoria led the way to the tall iron gates of the cemetery.

"This place is definitely haunted. You definitely wouldn't want to be here after dark. Once Sam Ferraro got chased by something. It made this deep, growling noise, and when he got home the back of his jacket had claw marks in it."

"You believe Sam?" said Nella. "He's just trying to get attention!"

Megan laughed. But you could tell the place made her nervous. "I'm not a graveyard fan," she said.

"Don't worry," said Victoria. "Nella's father works here. He'll protect us, right, Nella?"

"Your father works here?" Megan's eyelinered eyes went wide. "That is so gruesome. Does he dig graves?"

"No! He—"

"Oh my God, I get chills just thinking about it. What if the person's not really dead, and they wake up inside the coffin and start banging on the lid, but no one can hear them? They're already in the ground! Buried alive."

"That never happens!" cried Nella.

"I watched this show where they explained what happens to dead bodies. They ooze out this green slime and flesh-eating flies lay their eggs in it." Megan looked more excited than she had all day. "They can eat a whole entire corpse in like ten days."

"Not these corpses," said Nella. "They get embalmed. That stops them rotting."

"Wow." Megan grinned. "You're definitely a corpse expert."

"Death is the flip side of life." Dad always said that when people asked about his job. "It's a natural part of the cycle."

"Does he sleep in a coffin?" Megan asked, making Victoria dissolve into giggles. A second later, Kimmy did too.

"Don't be an idiot!" said Nella.

It was all over, she could tell. Whatever had made Victoria invite her wasn't going to last. If she'd had any sense, she'd have stomped away right then and avoided what happened next. But something stupid in her made her stand there, digging her stiff fingers deeper inside her pockets.

"Nella's father's pretty normal," Victoria blurted. "Except for the jail thing."

"Jail?" Now Megan really looked interested. "What'd he do?"

The wind was picking up. Nella's hands had gone numb. Her feet were lumps of ice attached to her legs. She couldn't move if she wanted to. She was a prisoner, waiting to hear her sentence read out.

"A car accident," Victoria said.

"He went to jail for a car accident?" Megan's brow wrinkled. "I think you're telling one of your whoppers, Vickie."

Victoria hesitated, like she was trying to decide something. With a sudden, quick twist of her shoulders, she made up her mind.

(Later, Nella would think the reason she hadn't run away was she wanted to hear. She wanted to hear what Victoria said next, to finally know this thing she'd suspected in some dark, buried part of her.)

"He hit a little girl and she died."

The ground shifted beneath Nella's feet. A crack opened wide, and she almost lost her balance. She had one foot here, one there. One in before, one in after. When she gasped, the air stayed cold in her mouth, in her throat, all the way down into her lungs.

"No!" It was a reflex, like holding up your hand when someone tried to slap you. "No."

"That's so terrible." Megan licked her lips. "That's like a huge, terrible tragedy. How old was the little girl?"

"Seven."

Kimmy pressed her mittens to her cheeks.

Vocabulary. The million stupid, useless words they'd learned. None of them fit this.

"Her whole life was ahead of her," Megan whispered. "Like how can he even live with himself?"

"How . . . how can *you*?" Nella flung the words into the empty air, where they hung for an instant and disappeared like smoke. She spun away, slipping on a patch of ice.

"How can he work in a cemetery? Isn't he scared vengeful ghosts will get him? Oh my God. Is *she* buried here?"

Nella ran, the cruel wind nipping her face, biting her heart.

He hit a little girl and she died.

What the Statue of Jeptha A. Stone Would Say if It Could

D ead is dead.

Another common misconception.

Hark unto me, Jeptha A. Stone. The dead live on in infinite ways. From beyond the grave, they comfort, they accuse. They nourish, they destroy. The reason ghosts do not exist is simple: they are not necessary.

For the living to be haunted, all that is required is a memory.

It is a fact that no living being remembers me.

Not that I mind, I hasten to add. Not at all. Not the least bit.

Monuments do not get lonely.

The very notion is undignified.

As is the feathered creature now nestled in my capacious lap. What a racket she and her chums make each dawn and dusk! You'd think they were trying to wake the dead.

YOU CAN'T ALWAYS GET
WHAT YOU WANT
now

The main reason people believed in God, Clem said, was they didn't want to feel alone. They wanted to believe Someone was watching over them. When Nella protested that there had to be Something Bigger than us in this world, Clem agreed. Of course there was!

"Music's bigger than us," she said. "Those emperor penguins that don't eat for a hundred and twenty days because they're faithfully guarding their eggs? They are colossal."

Nella liked penguins all right. But she could never pray to one.

Not that her prayers got results, anyway. No matter how many pleas and promises she made to heaven, the bishop didn't change his mind. At recess, Nella helped pack books into boxes that Sister Rosa labeled in her perfect handwriting. *First Grade Readers. Baltimore Catechisms.* The storage closet was so dusty, they both kept sneezing. Tears ran down their cheeks, and Sister dabbed them both with her endless supply of snow-white, rose-scented handkerchiefs.

"Are you all right?" Nella asked.

Sister's watery gaze wandered the shelves of books. She looked a little scared, as if it wasn't just books getting packed away. The other nuns had gotten new teaching assignments, but Sister Rosa was going to the rest home.

"Sometimes the Lord tests us," she said. "He wants to see what we're made of." She flexed a scrawny bicep. Sister had a scar over one eye, the same place as Anthony did. When she was little, she'd jumped out of a tree, certain she could fly. Now she smiled and patted Nella's arm. "His will be done."

Dad's favorite song had the line: "You can't always get what you want." The words sang inside Nella's head now. They seemed a lot like "His will be done," though it was probably a sin to think so.

IN COMMON
then

M urder. The worst, most unthinkable sin of all.

Nella slipped and slid down the hill from the cemetery, trying to escape Megan's words. Escape the look on Victoria's face. Did Kimmy already know too? Did everyone know except her?

Who could trust Victoria? Who'd believe that poisonous snake of a girl over Dad?

He'd graduated first in his high school class but mysteriously never gone to college.

Nella pitched forward, hands out, and landed on all fours. Scrambling up, she slipped again and this time fell on her butt. Peering over her shoulder, afraid the other girls were following and would laugh, instead she saw Angela.

"You look froze! Here." Angela pulled off a glove and gave it to Nella. They pushed their bare hands into their pockets. "Where are you going in such a rush?"

At home Nella's father would be watching the basketball game, the little brothers crawling over him like he was a human playground, while Salvatore sat upright and serious beside him, trying to be a Dad-replica. *Dad.* He was the sun. The center. Nella was sick. She leaned against the wall.

"Are you hurt?" Angela asked.

"Can I come to your house?"

By that time, they never went there anymore. But of course Angela said okay.

The DeMarcos' house had no smell. No smell of cooking, no dirty socks or baby spit-up or old-lady mildew. Even the air was afraid to offend Mr. DeMarco.

"Yo!" Anthony's head poked out of his room. "Secret sister!"

He held weights and curled one toward his chest. With another boy it would've looked manly and macho, but with Anthony it looked . . . silly. Nella giggled.

"Laugh at your own risk," he said. "Mock the Iron Man and suffer the consequences."

"Papa calls him a puny weakling," said Angela. "He says a girl could take Anthony down."

Anthony started doing push-ups. After half a minute his arms collapsed and his face mashed into the rug.

"Crap! Snap!"

Nella couldn't stop giggling. It felt weird, like parts of her were shaking loose. She was a tree and the wind was stripping off her leaves. Anthony and Angela stared at her.

"What's the matter?"

Nella tried to give her head a casual shake, but once she started shaking it she couldn't stop.

"Hey! Easy!" They sat on either side of her, bookends propping her up. "What's going on?"

"Victoria said my father killed a girl."

How could something so big—bigger than the whole world—fit into so few words?

She waited. Neither of them said anything. That was how Nella knew it was true.

"Talk to him," Anthony said at last. "He'll tell you what happened."

"But he won't! All this time he didn't!" Nella didn't want to cry. Crying would make it true all over again.

Anthony folded his hand over hers. It was the warm glove she'd been wishing for all day.

"He was trying to protect you," Anthony said.

"No! He was lying!"

Downstairs a door slammed.

"Anthony!" Mr. Demarco hollered. "Angela!"

Angela bolted to her feet. "You better go," she told Nella. "I can tell from his voice. You need to go."

Reluctantly, Nella drew her hand from Anthony's. She followed Angela out onto the landing.

"That stupid Victoria!" Angela made a face. "She's poison!"

"At least she told me the truth," Nella heard herself say. "Not like some people." Craziness roared up inside her. She let it. She didn't even try to stop it. "Why didn't you tell me? You . . . you jellyfish! You wimp!"

Downstairs, cupboard doors slammed. Angela gripped the railing. "Because," she said evenly, "it doesn't matter."

"Doesn't matter?" Nella wanted to push her. Push her right down the stairs. "You're so stupid I can't stand it!"

"What your father did, it's awful." Angela's mouth made a harsh, straight line. For a moment, Nella hardly recognized her. "But so what. It's too late. There's nothing you can do about it."

My father killed people. In the war.

This thing so terrible, it scared away words. This thing neither of their fathers would talk about. They had it in common.

P2F2
now

"According to the laws of physics," Clem said, "electrons and photons can occupy an *infinite* number of locations at the same time. All I'm asking for is *two*. Humans are composed of subatomic particles, so what is the problem? Why can't *we* be in two places at once?"

They were trudging up the hill after school. These trudges were numbered now. In less than a month, Clem and her parents would go away to Cape Cod, which was the inspiration for her ranting and raving.

"It's like time travel." She rummaged through her hair, making it stick up even more. Hedgehog Girl. "The physics support it, but when I ask my father why we still can't do it, he just laughs. *You* are *a time traveler,* he says. *You've traveled forward twelve years since I met you!*"

Clem paused to try to unhook a blue plastic bag caught in a sidewalk tree. She was too short, so Nella had to give her a boost. Victory! CRAPP was another of their two-member societies. Crusaders Raging Against Pukey Plastic.

Tomorrow they would take the magnet school admission test. Nella was definitely not thinking about that.

"Then he launches into wormholes and traveling at the speed of light and other inconvenient ways to move through space-time. And says someday we'll travel into the future, for sure." Clem stuffed the bag into the garbage pail outside Franny's. They paused again, this time to pay homage to the Sacred Scent of Doughnuts. "But travel to the past is more complicated and difficult, for some reason. Patch says we still can't grasp the science for that."

They reached Clem's door. Her spiky hair caught the light. Her glasses tilted on her nose. Even standing still, Clem was in motion. Hummingbird Girl.

"That's fine with me. I mean,

who'd want to go *backward* anyway?" Up on her toes, Clem cried, "Onward! GAD! Papaya juice and hedgehogs!"

"I can't. It's a Nonni afternoon."

Clem sank back down. She never offered to come to Nonni's, but who could blame her? It wasn't as if Nella made it sound like Fun Headquarters over there. Really, who could blame her one bit?

"So I'll see you tomorrow at the—"

"Don't say it. Just the word gives me a heart attack."

"I'll see you at the-thing-that-must-not-be-named. And afterward we'll plan the Leap Second celebration. Deal?"

"Deal."

Clem unlocked her door but didn't go inside. Her face turned suddenly, strangely anxious. What was happening? Clem never worried, except about things like whether there were other universes we'd never get to discover.

"Nell? Do you think you'll . . . We'll still be friends when I get back from the Cape, right?"

Nella took a step back. Clem had voiced her own fear, one that had lurked inside her since they first met. What if Clem got tired of her? What if Clem found a brainier, richer, more interesting friend? What if Clem finally realized they were the world's most unlikely friend combination?

(*Maybe this is how Angela felt.* The thought poked the

back of her brain. Weeks later, that thought would make its way to the very front.)

Never in a million years would Nella have guessed Clem worried about losing her.

"Forever," she said. "That's how long we'll be friends."

Clem grinned. "P2F2!" she cried.

Their newest secret society: Past Present Future Friends.

DAD'S SECRET
then

Nonni's kitchen clock was the old-fashioned kind that ticked. Nella sat at the table, which was covered with a plastic cloth meant to look like lace. Dad was here to fix Nonni's leaky faucet, and Nella had offered to keep him company. But that wasn't the real reason she'd come.

Tick-tock.

Nonni was in the living room, on guard by the window. She was playing a recording of her idol, Mario Lanza, who sang so high your teeth ached.

"Dad?"

He turned around, frowning. Nonni needed a new

faucet, but she was too cheap, so he just kept replacing washers.

Tick-tock.

"Dad?" She felt like she was on the edge of a cliff. "Dad, were you really in jail?"

His head jerked up.

"I heard . . . I heard these rumors," Nella said.

He looked at her a long moment, then crossed the kitchen and shut the door. He pulled out a chair.

"I was waiting till you were old enough to understand," he said.

Most of the time, Nonni's clock ticked so quietly, you didn't notice. But every once in a while, the ticking ramped up. *Tick tick tick,* so loud you couldn't ignore it. The clock wanted you to pay attention. These seconds were important.

It did that now.

"I'm old enough," she said. "I've been old enough."

Dad looked at her for a long moment, then lowered his eyes.

"I'm sorry, Nella," he said.

Falling. Nella was falling.

Dad kept his eyes on the tablecloth as he talked.

It was May third, he said. A Saturday. That morning, he got the letter saying he'd won a scholarship to the university at the top of the hill. He'd been accepted weeks before but couldn't afford to go. He ran straight to Elena's Beauty Shop, where Nonni and Ernestina were getting their hair done. Nonni burst into happy tears. All the women in the shop hugged and kissed him. Afterward, he stunk of curling lotion.

The day was warm and bright. Word spread fast, and as Dad walked through the neighborhood, everyone shook his hand, clapped him on the back. Bravo! King of the Hill! It was First Communion Day, and the little kids were getting their pictures taken on the church steps. All in white, head to toe. Like a little band of angels, he said.

He kept his eyes on the table.

The clock ticked.

That afternoon, he and his buddies celebrated. They got somebody's older brother to buy them six-packs and headed into the cemetery, in section 58. Those days, the plots back there were still unoccupied. He'd forgotten to eat lunch, and as he sat in the sunshine, the beer went right to his head. Looking around, he knew he'd be the first man in the family to escape working in a graveyard.

It was the best he'd ever felt in his entire life.

Dad fell asleep on the grass, and when he woke up, his buddies were gone. Had he dreamed the whole thing? He dug in his pocket, and pulled out the letter. Real. It was real.

Something else was in his pocket, too. The keys to

Nonni and PopPop's enormous Buick LeSabre. Dad had driven Nonni to her doctor's appointment the day before and still had the spare set of keys.

Nonni. Dad needed to do something to show how much he loved and appreciated her. He'd get her chocolate. No, flowers. No, he'd drive up the hill to that fancy grocery store and get her persimmons. Nonni loved to tell about the persimmon tree that grew behind their house in Italy. She and her brother, Carlo, would climb up, spoons between their teeth, and gobble the luscious fruit till their bellies burst.

Sitting at the kitchen table now, Nella nodded. She'd heard about that persimmon tree.

Dad had no business driving, after all that beer. But he'd gotten it in his head to buy Nonni persimmons, and from now on, he was going to have whatever he wanted. King of the World.

It wasn't persimmon season. He went to three or four stores before he gave up and bought artichokes. A whole boxful.

"Nonni hates artichokes," Nella said. Her great-grandmother refused to even look at the things. "They make her sick."

"Before," he said. "Before, she loved them."

The clock hushed.

Dad didn't remember driving back from the store. By then, he could hardly keep his eyes open. Maybe he nodded off for a second—he'd never be sure. That enormous tank of a car, hurtling down the hill.

"All I remember is something white." He jerked his head sideways, like he'd suddenly seen it again. "Pure white, like a snowflake. Like a white pinwheel. It blinded me. For a split second, it was the only thing I could see. And then, gone. It was gone."

His eyes met Nella's. Then he quickly looked up at the clock.

"She'd made her First Communion that morning. She and her family were coming out of Mama Gemma's, where they'd gone to celebrate."

There was a thin smear of jelly on the fake lace tablecloth. Nella's head swam. On her own First Communion day, he couldn't get out of bed. He couldn't even look at her in her white dress. Her father stared hard at the clock, like he was trying to make the hands go backward.

"They could've stayed in the restaurant a little longer. Or left earlier." He shoved back his chair. "I could've put the car keys back, instead of believing I could have whatever I wanted."

Dad went to the sink and stood there a long moment.

"I did two years," he said, his back to her. "The judge went easy on me, since I was an honor student with no record." He picked up the wrench and put it back down. "Nonni came to see me every single Sunday. She never missed."

Nella could picture her: straight-backed, grim-faced. A match for the toughest prison guard.

"She never blamed me, not once. She asked me what happened and I told her, and we never talked about it again. Even when PopPop died, six months later. They've proven it's true—people really can die of a broken heart."

Nella traced the pattern of the plastic lace with one finger, over and over. Where had her own heart gone? She couldn't feel it inside her anymore.

"You know she never learned to drive. After he died, she had to take three buses to come see me, but she never missed. I watched her grow old right before my eyes, Nella. I felt like I was killing somebody else, only this time in slow motion."

Dad stared out the window over the sink.

"The first Sunday after I got out, she dragged me to Mass. I wasn't ready to face people, but she made me. Somebody must've said something behind my back. Next thing I knew she clipped the guy in the ear with that black purse. The same one she's still got." He shook his head, gave a low chuckle. Another moment passed. "Getting hired is almost impossible with a record. But Nonni pulled strings and got me the groundskeeper job."

Nella knew what came next. How one night Dad met Mom at the social club. How she was the most beautiful woman he'd ever seen. How, when he proposed, he never dreamed she'd say yes.

And Nella was born, and all the boys, and here they were, in Nonni's kitchen. The story made a lopsided circle.

"I kept promising your mother I'd tell you. She said you'd understand. But . . ." He turned around, his face brimming with regret. "I never really knew my father. And PopPop—he was the kindest, most trustworthy man who ever lived. I wish you'd known him, kiddo. That's the kind of dad I always thought I'd be."

"That's the kind of dad I thought you were."

The anger in Nella's voice shocked them both. Her father flattened his back against the sink.

"I should've told you, Nella. I'm sorry."

Somebody had stolen her dad and set this other man in his place. The person in front of her was a stranger. A separate, foreign person from the father she'd spent her whole life loving and trusting and believing in more than anyone on earth.

"I'm sorry it happened. Sorry I had to hurt you like this." He looked away, then back. "I'll be sorry for the rest of my life."

He was waiting for her to say something. She saw the pleading in his eyes. The clock hushed, waiting. She could go to him and press her cheek against his chest. She could say she knew it was an accident, he never meant it, he would never hurt anyone, it was all right that he hadn't told her, she understood. Nothing was changed. She still loved him. With just a few words, she could erase everything.

Tick tick tick. The clock stuttered forward.

He'd kept it secret from her all these years! How could he do that? She'd thought the two of them didn't need to talk, that they understood each other without any words. Instead, all this time he'd been deceiving her.

"Is the girl . . . is she buried in your cemetery?"

"Marie. Her name was Marie. Yes, she is."

Dad waited a moment longer, then slowly turned back to the sink. He worked the wrench in silence. When Nella said she was going home, he only nodded.

Instead of home, Nella went to the cemetery. She looked for a young girl's grave, marked with the name Marie.

What the Statue of
Jeptha A. Stone
Would Say if It Could

Although she had her pick of any spot in this vast, lush landscape, the bird has chosen to nest in my lapidarian lap.

To all appearances, she is a foolish fowl.

Hark unto me, the Honorable Jeptha A. Stone!

More often than not, appearances deceive.

Besides. Have you ever tried to argue with a bird?

MARIE
then

All that spring, Nella searched for Marie's grave. STONE. BRIDGE. KING. WADE. HUNT. She tromped past the graves of the rich, powerful people the cemetery was made for. Their names were sharp and quick, like karate chops. The graves of the people who built the cemetery—people like PopPop, with soft, chewy last names—were on the edges, what Dad called less prime real estate.

The cemetery was busy in spring. Nella walked past art school students photographing the monuments with complicated cameras, past straw-hatted garden club women oohing and ahhing over Daffodil Hill, past mothers pushing strollers and a couple lying on a blanket in the glossy shade of a copper beech. She walked past people with clasped hands and bowed heads, people on their knees praying.

For Nella, the cemetery had always been a peaceful, orderly place, but that spring it was different. She scrutinized the name on each grave. Each was a real, flesh-and-blood person who'd worked and played, laughed and cried, and never wanted to die.

For the first time, she wondered what it was like, really like, to die.

You'd gasp for breath but it wouldn't be there. Your eyes would be open but you wouldn't see.

For the first time, she understood why, beautiful as the cemetery was, plenty of people refused to set foot inside.

Last place on earth I'd go! That was another graveyard joke.

What was it like to kill someone? To watch the life ebb out of them and know it was because of you?

That was as hard to imagine as dying yourself.

One afternoon that spring, Nella sat at the kitchen table watching Mom cut up apples. One second they were whole, and the next they were pieces that could never be put back together.

That spring, the whole world felt like that.

Her father wasn't who she thought he was. Who he'd made her believe he was. He'd made Mom promise not to tell, and she hadn't. Mom. Somehow Nella couldn't be angry at her. All Mom wanted was for them to be happy. She loved them all so much, almost too much.

He'd turned Nella into a liar too. Because she couldn't tell the brothers. She saw how they ran to him, how they adored him, and the words stuck in her throat.

So many of the old graves were children's. Babies'. Nella hoped they'd been baptized, so they could go straight to heaven.

Did Marie have brothers and sisters?

She could've asked her father where the grave was. Instead, as she searched, she kept an eye out for him. If she heard an ATV or weed whacker, she headed in the opposite direction. After that day in Nonni's kitchen, neither of them ever mentioned Marie. The more time went by, the more talking about it became impossible.

That spring, Nella and Angela gave up Franny's doughnuts for Lent, and it was even more terrible than they expected.

That spring, Victoria and Kimmy specialized in behind-the-hand whispering that stopped the moment Nella came near. Victoria had a sleepover that got discussed for days before and after. Victoria braided Kimmy's hair, and Kimmy walked around at recess sucking on the tips.

Sister Rosa knew something was wrong. She let Nella and Angela stay in at recess. She gave them homemade brownies, and told the story of how in high school, smack in the middle of a school dance, she realized she wanted to be a nun.

"I was having such a good time. And dancing with a very handsome fellow." Her face was all dimples, till she shrugged. "All of a sudden, I knew. It was all wrong for me."

"What was all wrong?"

"All . . . that." Sister fluttered her hand at the wide world. "I heard a voice calling me, heard it more clearly and irresistibly than the dance music or my handsome beau's laughter. My heart leaped to answer!" Sister sat back and smiled at them. "When I asked my fellow to take me home, I was as surprised as he was. Now I know. God seeks us out. Even when we try to hide, He still finds us."

That afternoon, Nella walked all the way to the edge of the cemetery, where the landscape turned wilder. Moss crept over these stones, hard as Dad worked to keep them clean. The trees were thick, the light itself pale green. Rustles, whispers, sighs disturbed the air. People who believed in ghosts did not walk back here.

Rounding a bend in the path, she saw the statue of a

young girl. She was on her toes, one arm stretched upward. Her face tilted toward the sky. Every inch of her yearned. *Yearned.*

Her name was carved in the base.

MARIE MAGELLAN

CHILD OF LIGHT

Nella sank onto a stone bench thick with pollen and grit. No one must have sat here for a long time. In the whispering air, the girl kept reaching for something invisible.

"You died in a state of grace," Nella said softly. "You went straight to heaven. Marie? Can you look down and see me?"

A small, yellow-flecked bird lighted on the girl's lifted hand. It sang three sweet, rising notes, tra la la, then flew away.

It wasn't till she got home that Nella realized it was May 3, the day Marie died.

AIUTA!
now

Wet bags drooped from the trees like vampire bats. Nella had surreptitiously borrowed the long-handled claw thing Nonni used for reaching things she dropped. Once she was armed with this mighty weapon, no piece of pukey plastic could defeat the CRAPP.

Invincible, Nella and Clem bought lemon ices from Terraci's, then ate them sitting on the steps of the church. This morning, they had taken the magnet school admission test. They definitely were not talking about it.

"My mother took Vinny for a checkup this week, and the doctor said he recommends a neurologist."

"Einstein didn't talk till he was three."

"So maybe Vinny's a genius?"

"Maybe on his third birthday he'll say, *I have unlocked the mystery of dark matter.*"

"Or maybe *This family is certifiably crazy.*"

They passed the souvenir shop. In Nella's pocket was the stolen scarf, which she'd brought to the test as a good-luck charm. This was how pathetic she was. The admission test had been so hard, her brain was still gasping like a hooked fish.

It wasn't like she wanted to go to a math-and-science magnet school anyway. Nella was terrible at math and didn't care about science. Girls were not supposed to say things like that anymore, but it was the truth.

All she wanted was to stay with Clem.

She tripped.

"Invisible gnome alert!" Clem laughed and pushed her new glasses up her nose. The lenses were even thicker than the last pair. Nella kept growing clumsier and Clem kept growing blinder. The clouds parted, turning the rain-washed air all silvery.

"Did I tell you what Bobby did? He dropped Legos in the cake batter. My father chipped a tooth."

But Clem was distracted. She scratched her head with the claw.

"There's no known law of physics that says time has to run forward. But it always does. It never reverses. Time always moves toward the next thing, not the last. It's like the future is . . . irresistible." She spun to face Nella. "The Leap Second I was telling you about? The extra second they're adding to the clock in August? Remember?"

"Umm . . ."

"Okay, listen. To stay in synch with the Earth's rotation, sometimes they have to fiddle with how we keep time. So this August, we get a free extra second of future. Think about it. It's a colossal gift. Nell, we can't waste it. We need to catch that special second and make it officially ours. Clem and Nell, Time Sisters!"

Holding the claw at arm's length, Clem marched like a drum majorette. They reached the top of the hill and the gates to the university campus. Hung between two massive stone columns, they loomed heavy and important, just like the gates to the cemetery. Clem gave back the claw and headed for her father's lab.

Maybe time never reversed, but Nella had to. Pulling the scarf out of her pocket and looping it around her neck, she retraced her footsteps down the hill to Nonni's.

Who sat on her porch, wearing her black sweater buttoned to her chin, a plastic visor, and the giant sunglasses they gave her last time she went to the eye doctor. Not exactly a relaxed, springtime look. Dad had un-burlapped the fig tree, and its leaves glowed with green gratitude. Adjusting her Kryptonite-deflecting sunglasses, Nonni pointed across the street.

"No like."

Bright purple curtains billowed in the upstairs window. Today, the music was dazzling as a skipping stone. On the porch a girl with one of those red dots on her forehead sat reading.

"Gypsies!"

"No, Nonni. She's a student at the college up the hill."

"Baby snatchers!"

"I'm going to make you some lunch."

When she came back with a sandwich, Hairy Boy was hopping off his bike, dashing inside. A moment later, the music stopped midsong. Nella imagined him and Turtle Girl kissing. He'd hold her face between his hands. She'd go up on her toes to meet his hungry lips. Imagining it, Nella tottered. Her head bumped into a hanging pot. Her body had grown again without her permission. A stealth body, that's what she occupied.

Who would ever love her? A clumsy, pimply skyscraper of a girl like her?

Nonni curled her lip at the sandwich and pointed to

the mailbox. When Nella lifted the top, she found a bag of Laffy Taffy. The candy sometimes stuck in her dentures, but Nonni still loved it.

"Where does the general put his armies?" she read.

Nonni leaned forward expectantly. She loved Laffy Taffy jokes.

"In his sleevies!"

Nonni slapped the arms of her chair and laughed that crazy big laugh. As Nella handed her the candy, a sudden memory flitted across her mind: Nonni feeding baby-her a bite of perfectly ripe fig.

Hairy Boy dashed back outside, jumped on his bike, and pedaled away. Did he just stop by to steal a quick, passionate kiss? His hair flapped like a great, hairy sail. The music started up again, even brighter and more dazzling. It coaxed the sun to shine brighter, the fig tree to release a hint of delicious figgy perfume.

Nonni's fingers suddenly pinched Nella's arm so hard she yelped.

A uniformed man was walking by. He had close-cropped blond hair and wore a black shirt with an emblem on the sleeve, a shiny badge on the pocket. A black belt with unfriendly things buckled on. Nella's heart lurched. Anthony! She knew he was a security guard now, but she'd never seen him in uniform.

"Stop him!" Nonni was amputating Nella's arm. *"Aiuto!"* Help!

Anthony looked up. That familiar smile. Nella's heart did a cartwheel.

"Nella-smella-marshamella!" He climbed the porch steps. "Mrs. Sabatini."

"Anthony!" Nonni pressed her hands together in prayer. *"Grazie a Dio!* You're police now?"

Nella rolled her eyes, and Anthony gave her a wink. Pulling a pad from his back pocket, he propped his foot on the porch railing and pretended to take notes as Nonni complained about the Invaders out to steal her money. (What money? Nonni never stopped lamenting how she didn't have two nickels to rub together.)

What Anthony was really doing, Nella saw, was sketching. The alien sunglasses, the plastic visor, the bony cheeks—it was Nonni, but improved. Anthony took that old face and made it fierce and brave, almost the face of someone you'd want to know. His hands moved quickly and easily, his deep-set eyes barely glancing at the paper.

But his hair was clipped so short it bristled instead of curling. And his arms, once so scrawny, were muscular. Nella felt uneasy. This wasn't her Anthony, the one who drew her castles and unicorns. The gentleness was sandpapered away, leaving behind something raw. Suddenly, she felt afraid for him.

"*Gitani!*" Nonni whispered. *Gypsies.*

Turtle Girl, instrument case on her back, butter-yellow scarf around her neck, stepped outside. She paused, giving them a questioning look.

"See?" hissed Nonni. "*Male.*" *Evil.*

Turtle Girl frowned. What if she crossed the street and demanded that Nonni quit harassing them? Nella would die of mortification.

That was when she remembered she was wearing the stolen scarf.

The girl furrowed her brow. Nella slid down in her chair. She yanked the scarf off and stuffed it in her pocket. But the girl wasn't looking at her. It was Anthony making her frown. She didn't approve of men with badges and uniforms and unfriendly-looking belts. Nella's cheeks grew warm. What did that girl know? Just because she was a college student, with a cute boyfriend and dainty feet and who knew how many silk scarves, what did she know? Did she know what a great artist Anthony was, or how much he loved his little sister, or that his father loyally served their country? No, she did not. After a moment, the girl turned on her heel and walked away.

A turtle, protected by her shell.

Anthony rubbed the scar above his eye. He looked sad and squashed. He looked, Nella realized, like that stiff uniform was wearing him, not the other way around.

"She's just a dumb ignorant student," she said.

Now Nonni started talking about PopPop's brother, Vito, who was a mounted policeman. He'd take the nieces and nephews to the stables and let them feed the horses apples. *Molto grande. Huge*—those horses were huge. Their hooves were the size of a newborn's head. Vito and his horse stood guard when the coloreds made that riot down at the bottom of the hill. He was there, on his powerful horse, making sure they didn't cross the line into this neighborhood. And when they bused their kids into the old school, Vito and the others were there, letting those people know: no one wanted them here. They did not belong here.

Nonni told these stories when she got really worked up. Nella didn't know how much was true, how much was old-lady craziness. Once she'd asked Mom, but her mother had told her she didn't need to worry about things that happened before she was born, things nobody was proud of. The past was the past, Mom said.

And then grew quiet, as if she knew that wasn't always true.

Anthony was frowning now, sliding his notebook back into his pocket.

"With all due respect, Mrs. S," he said, "times have changed."

Nonni's look turned uncertain. Anthony dipped his head.

"It's all right," he said. "You're safe now, okay?"

Nella followed him out to the sidewalk. Making people feel safe—now it was his official job, but it had always been who he was. Watching over Angela. For years, watching over her, too.

For the first time she wondered, who was watching over him?

Anthony hooked a finger in his belt. Was one of those things a gun? Looking at him again, she saw she was wrong. He wasn't sad and squashed. He was angry. Furious. Beneath those new muscles, deep inside, something was coiled up tight.

(Later, she would remember that.)

"She seems kind of shaky," he said.

"Who?" Confused, for a moment she thought he meant Angela.

"Your great-grandmother, that's who." Anthony gave her a funny look. Then he ruffled her head like she was a silly puppy, and that was the last she saw of him, till long after it happened.

ANTHONY'S SECRET
then

Anthony won a scholarship to take classes at the art school. He kept up his part-time after-school job too, so Nella hardly ever saw him.

Mr. DeMarco got into a fistfight at Mama Gemma's. He was banned from there now. Also the social club. About the only place he was welcome these days was church, and he hardly ever showed up.

That summer, the summer after fourth grade, Anthony fell in love.

Her name was Janelle Johnson. He met her at the art school, Angela said, swearing Nella to secrecy. One afternoon they followed Anthony up the hill, past the university gates, down a street lined with cute shops, to the corner where Janelle waited. Nella and Angela hid behind a tall sidewalk planter and watched him kiss her hello. Janelle's eyes were dark and shiny, like plums dipped in water.

Hate was a sin. But Nella hated Janelle.

"Why do they sneak around?" she hissed. "What's their problem? It's stupid. It's dumb."

"You know why," Angela said.

Nella pretended not to. "Because she's black, you mean?"

Angela looked away. "You can't tell anyone. We have to protect them."

They crossed pinkies and touched all four fingertips together. The Secret Sister Sign.

Someone else ratted to Mr. DeMarco. Angela suspected Kenny Lombardo, that meathead. *Ballistic* was too feeble a word for Mr. DeMarco. He took away Anthony's phone. He threw his drawing supplies in the garbage. He said he'd rather have a son who was a retard or a homo than a liar and a sneak. He went insane, even for him.

"So did Anthony," Angela said.

They sat on the playground swings. The rusty chains left orange powder on their hands.

"He called Papa names I never even heard of. And I've heard plenty. Then he slammed out." Angela twisted her swing. "Papa locked the doors. He said if I let Anthony in, I'd be sorry."

As much as Nella hated Janelle, she hated this story more.

"After he went to bed, I unlocked the door. In the morning, Anthony was in the kitchen, making eggs. His face was like this."

Angela's face went slack and rigid at the same time. Her eyes emptied out, and she was a zombie.

"Don't! You're creeping me out!" cried Nella.

"Anthony said he was sorry. Papa didn't say it, but he acted like it. Then they had this long talk, and Anthony promised as soon as he graduates he'll get a job."

"But he's supposed to go to art school!"

Angela twisted her swing tighter.

"Papa said he wants us to be safe and secure. Anthony said he knows all the sacrifices Papa made, and he wants to make Papa proud. They both got tears in their eyes. Even though real men never cry."

Nella looked down at her hands, coated rusty orange.

"Papa made Anthony eat the extra bacon. It was the first time we were like a real family since . . . forever."

Angela tucked her feet up and let go. Head down, she

spun in a tight, fast circle. Nella had to look away—just watching made her dizzy-sick. Angela stuck out her foot. Stop.

"Anthony came back on account of me. Otherwise, he'd run away and marry Janelle and be an artist."

"He didn't have to come back." How many times had Sister Rosa told them they had free will? "He wanted to."

"No he didn't. He hated to." Angela's face was dizzy-pale. "But he did."

What the Statue of Jeptha A. Stone Would Say if It Could

This morning an artiste photographed me and my bird. Ahem. *The* bird.

I daresay that arty woman found the sight of us quite amusing.

Could I have spoken, here is what I would have told her:

Hark unto me, Jeptha A. Stone! First of all, laughing at the plight of another is a sign of low breeding and coarse character.

Second of all, the true test is not what we choose for ourselves. It is how we deal with what life chooses for us.

Meanwhile, my bird sings. She sings the sun up in the morning and down in the evening. If one could see her song, it would be a pure, golden ring hovering in the air. A halo. Proof of goodness.

Ahem.

THE FUTURE AWAITS
now

The school was up for sale. It was being converted into more condos. Or a performance art space. Or a wellness center, with yoga classes and a juice bar.

"Pedicures and massages in our classrooms?" said Nella. "That would be so wrong."

"My mom gets massages all the time," said Clem. "Afterward I can ask her for the moon and she'll say why not."

Clem didn't much care what happened to the school. She wasn't worried about Sister Rosa. She wasn't attached the same way Nella was—how could she be? Nella didn't hold it against her. Not at all. Not a single bit.

On the very last day forever, Nella got to school early. The playground was empty. Wait. No it wasn't.

"Hi." Angela stood beside the statue of St. Amphibalus. The spot where they first met. In Another Life.

"Hi."

Walking away would be so awkward. Nella studied the flowers planted beside St. A. They badly needed water.

"I was thinking something really weird," Angela said.

Remember the first day of kindergarten? When we didn't have a clue, and Anthony tied your shoes, and it all began?

If anyone in the universe understood how Nella felt right now, it was Angela DeMarco.

"An-ge-la!" A stampede of abominations. They immediately commenced showing off—throwing rocks, hawking goobers, pulling up shirts to display mosquito bites. Why did they think this would make Angela love them? All these years Nella had lived with boys, and the blueprint of their minds remained a mystery.

Angela poked Bobby in the armpit, the most ticklish place on his hyperticklish body, and he curled up like a sow bug. Kevin picked her a bouquet of dandelions. Nella saw how much they missed her, and a light switched on in some dim, unused room of her mind. Angela must miss them just as much. It wasn't only Nella she used to visit.

It was Mom, it was the brothers. It was the loud, tangled, anything-goes mess of them all together. Nella's toe scuffed the edge of the flower patch. Her thoughts skittered away from Angela's silent land mine of a house.

"What?" she asked Angela. "What something really weird?"

"Never mind."

"Please tell me."

"You know that saying, if only these walls could talk, the stories they'd tell? I was thinking, what if this statue could talk? All these years, he's stood here watching kids run around and play and . . . you know. Grow up. He might have some interesting things to say."

The brothers loved this. They told Angela she was cuckoo, she was mental, her elevator skipped a few floors. Statues couldn't see! Statues couldn't hear or talk!

"I told you it was weird." Angela gave the smile that turned her into a yellow-haired princess in a tower. "But I'm worried about what will happen to him now."

Kids began piling in from all sides. The last day! It was the last day forever. Flannel shirt flapping like a cape, Clem skidded up on her banana bike. Angela slipped across the school yard to stand beside Ellen Romano, who was repeating sixth grade and had breasts as big as Nella's mother's. Sam and his friends threw an imaginary football, hug-tackled each other. So much energy and commotion, it was impossible to believe it could be the end of anything. Nella looked up into St. A's humble eyes. What would he say if he could?

It wasn't a weird thing to wonder. She wanted to know too. She wished she'd told Angela that.

That afternoon, while scrubbing desks, Nella went for more paper towels. Sam followed her. He'd pulled off his school tie, already finished with uniforms.

"So? Where you going next year?"

"I'm weighing my options." She bent her knees. Imperceptibly, she hoped.

"Well, I'm *definitely* going to Garfield. In case that helps you make up your mind."

"You mean, about where I *definitely* don't want to go?"

Grinning, he grabbed the roll of towels and held it out of her reach. He followed her back into the room, bopping her on the head with it.

"Oh, mature," Nella said, her face a bonfire. "Extremely mature."

"Told you," said Clem out of the corner of her mouth.

And then, just like that, it was all over. Now became then. Sister Rosa stood at the door to say good-bye to each of them. Nella worried her old bones would wear out from all the hugging. She could hardly stand to look at Sister. She couldn't believe they'd never see each other again in this world.

In the cemetery stood little houses, some built into the side of the hill and some standing free, all with heavy grates over the doors. Inside were "remains." Vaults, the buildings were called, and that was what the school already felt like, a locked-up vault of memories.

Outside, clouds hung heavy in the sky. Everyone's backpack was empty.

St. Amphibalus watched in frozen astonishment.

What's going on here? Where are you all going? You're not deserting me, are you?

"The future awaits!" Ninja Clem spun, leaped, and punched the air. "The universe is ours for the conquering!"

She threw a kick. Sam Ferraro laughed, just as the clouds opened up and sudden rain poured down. They ran for their lives.

BECAUSE ANGELA
DIDN'T TELL, AGAIN
then

Fifth grade was a year when everything only became more what it already was.

Nella got taller yet. Mom had another baby. Nonni grew even more intolerable, though how could that be possible?

A few days before sixth grade started, Nella and Angela went down the hill to Value Variety. The summer had been cool and rainy but now it turned steamy hot, the way it always did just before school started. Nella had pimples on her nose. Her hair was a frizz disaster. Angela was walking even more slowly than usual, which was so irritating, Nella strode ahead, not waiting. Till Angela said something that made her stop and turn around.

"What? What did you say?"

"He can start the training in a few weeks, as soon as he's eighteen. And he says he's guaranteed a job the minute he finishes."

"Anthony? A security guard? That's not right."

"I know!" Angela looked miserable. "What if something happens? What if he gets shot or stabbed or somebody beats him up?"

Nella pictured Anthony alone in a dark, empty building, shouting, *Halt! Who's there?* A man lunged out of the darkness and grabbed Anthony by the throat.

"Will he have a gun?" she asked.

Angela's pink hoodie was too big—why was she even wearing it, in this heat? She pushed up its sleeves, which immediately flopped back down.

"He says it's not dangerous at all but I know he's just saying that. What if something happens to him, Nella?"

"It can't. It won't. And . . . he'll have a gun, right?"

"He hates guns. He's always making sure Papa's is locked up safe."

"Your father has a gun?"

"You have to pray for Anthony. Every night, pray for him, okay?"

"Okay."

They crossed their pinkies and touched all four fingertips.

(Later, Nella would blame herself for not praying harder.)

They still weren't supposed to go to Value Variety, or anywhere else in this neighborhood. But Nella wanted nail polish, and where else was she supposed to get it? That afternoon, the store was packed with stuff and people. There was summer clearance, back-to-school, Halloween, and even some Christmas decorations. Binders, notebooks, and packs of markers were scattered on the floor. A display of snack cakes had toppled over. "Uh-oh," said a baby riding by in a shopping cart. "Uh-oh!"

Nella and Angela studied the million colors of nail polish. The store wanted it to be impossible for you to make up your mind.

"I want all of them," Nella said, making Angela laugh. But Nella wasn't really joking. The store was full of stuff to want. *Me want, me want.* Cookie Monster's voice croaked in her head. "If I had ten, I could do every finger a different color."

"You know you only have enough money for two. I'll help you pick. We'll narrow them down."

Angela's own nails, as usual, were bitten to the quick,

and as usual, she had no money. Nella couldn't stop thinking about Anthony. Being a security guard was all wrong. What if he never got to be an artist? She pictured his heart like one of those farm fields in a drought, dry and brown, with withered tufts sticking up from the cracks.

"Remember when Anthony stole those Disaster Dolls?" she said. "Can you believe he did that for us?"

Angela didn't answer. She selected two different shades of blue and held them up.

"Security guards catch shoplifters," said Nella. "Isn't that weird?"

"I don't want to talk about it. Come on. Pick."

"Wait. I just thought of something. Do you think he still steals? The bracelets and things he gives you?"

Angela looked shocked. "No, I do not think that. He'd never." But now she looked anxious.

"He would. He'd do anything for you. Even break the law."

"Don't be crazy. Now pay attention. Which one do you like better?"

Some college kids strolled by, laughing, their arms brimming with clothes hangers and detergent and rolled-up posters. (Was Hairy Boy with them that day? Turtle Girl? Nella wouldn't have recognized them, not yet.) Usually the students fascinated Nella, but today the sight of them made her angry. They didn't even know how lucky they were.

"Oh my God, it's freaking arctic in this store," one of them said, and Nella realized she was shivering, too.

Angela held up two shades of green polish. Who knew what happened next? Nella's brain slipped some important gear. Blindly, she grabbed the bottles from Angela and dropped them into her pocket. Angela's eyes bulged. She went into statue mode, her empty hands frozen in the air, as Nella swiped two more.

"Take some! Pull your sleeves over your hands." Who said that? Not Nella. Someone else had taken over. The reaching girl, the girl who wanted everything she couldn't have.

"Nella, don't!"

"It's not fair you have no money! This place is so crowded. Go on! No one will notice."

Nella started toward the doors. Her heart scrabbled and scratched inside her like it had grown claws. Her legs wanted to run, but now she remembered Anthony strolling the aisles, casual as could be. Maybe she *was* going crazy, but she felt like Anthony was showing her what to do. *Act natural,* she told herself, and prayed Angela, close behind her, had the sense to do the same.

The checkout lines stretched all the way back to the

greeting cards. Maybe she should buy something, even something small, to look less suspicious. Anthony had bought bread that day. Her hands shook as she reached for a magazine, and she knew she couldn't do it. She had to get out of here, right away. Right now.

The automatic door opened, and sunshine threw itself in her face. She spun around to tell Angela *Don't run till we're across the street*, but it wasn't Angela behind her. Someone else, a girl with tattoos, was so close she bumped into Nella.

"Whoa! Excuse," the girl said, and kept on going.

Panic rose inside her. Where was Angela? What happened? She pressed her palms to the front windows, trying to see between the signs plastered on the glass. Crowds of shoppers. Where was she? Nella moved back to the door. It flew open, making her jump away, and another stranger hurried out.

Angela stood just inside. A scowling man in an ugly tie had her by the sleeve of her pink hoodie. He was talking to her, but Angela refused to look at him. Her face was empty, no fear, no regret or pleading—every emotion was scrubbed off. It was the face she'd made that day on the playground swings, the blank, rigid, zombie expression that freaked Nella out. The face she said Anthony put on for their father.

Nella drew a sharp breath, and Angela turned her head. Their eyes met.

She would point. She would cry, *Her! It was all her idea!* The man would nab Nella and drag her inside too.

Instead, Angela raised her eyebrows, so pale they were almost invisible. Her head gave a tiny jerk. *Go! Run!* The door swung shut.

Astonished, for a moment Nella couldn't move. Then, without knowing how, she was walking, she was running. The bottles of nail polish clicked together in her pocket, loud as gunshots in her ears.

Louder still was the thought inside her head: *Angela saved me.*

Safely across the street, she stopped. Time stopped, too. What were they doing to her? Did they call her father? Nella's mind blurred with fear. She couldn't think of anything worse.

But like Nonni said, bad could always get worse. A police car pulled up. An officer went inside, and Nella watched him come out with Angela. He held the car's back door open as she got in, her face a blank sheet.

Nella couldn't sleep. When Vinny woke fussing, she got up and lifted him from his crib. Her mother staggered in, but Nella said she'd walk him. She was wide awake.

Up and down, in and out of the unnaturally quiet rooms. It had been the world's stupidest idea. If only she'd stopped to think! She went back to the moment she still held the bottles of nail polish. She made herself walk to the checkout and pay. She made the two of them walk back here, where they gave each other manicures.

She tried telling herself it wasn't really her fault.

"I never meant to get her in trouble," she whispered in her brother's pink ear. He grabbed a fold of her T-shirt and sucked it. "And she didn't have to do it. I didn't make her."

She stopped by the front window. The streetlight threw a cone of light against the cemetery wall.

"It was her own free choice," Nella whispered.

Vinny nestled into the hollow beneath her chin. Nella closed her eyes and made herself march back inside the store. She squared her shoulders, stepped up to the red-faced manager, and proclaimed, *I'm the one to blame, not her!*

It would have been the right thing to do.

A rush of shame. She saw Angela jerk her chin sideways. *Run, Nella!*

Angela was a jellyfish. A wimp. She was such a goody-goody, she was asking to get picked on. That's what everyone said. That's how everyone saw her.

But she had saved Nella.

All that evening Nella had waited for Mr. DeMarco to call and inform her parents: *Your daughter is a criminal. Not only that. She corrupted Angela. Not only that. She ran away and let Angela take all the punishment.* Every ring of the phone was a hammer to her heart—but he never called.

Vinny's warm, sleepy breath tickled her ear. Nella leaned her forehead against the dark window. The craziest thing of all was that somehow, it felt like she'd done it for Anthony. Like, if he couldn't have what he wanted, she could. Life was unfair, so you had to snatch what you wanted. You had to break some rules.

Crazy. Crazy crazy crazy. Anthony wouldn't want anything to do with her, once he found out. Betraying Angela was betraying him, only worse. He'd never forgive her getting his sister in such big trouble. He'd never again tease her about being his other little sister, never draw a castle and say *Here's where Princess Nella lives*, never surprise her with a slice of Mama Gemma's sausage-and-olive, her favorite. Never rub the scar over his eye and tell her to think for herself. Never, never.

Next morning, her head was a block of wood. Her eyes itched. She and Angela stood together beside St. Amphibalus, their seventh first day of school together. All around them, giddy kids ran and yelled and fist-bumped. Angela told Nella she had to put the nail polish back. Nella had to sneak into the store and return them to the shelf. Nella nodded her wooden head. She said she was sorry, over and over again.

"What did your father do?"

"You know what?" Angela said. "I don't want to talk about it."

Nella recognized that stubborn voice. It was no use asking again. Anyway, Nella didn't really want to know. Except, when you didn't know, you imagined the worst things possible. St. Amphibalus gazed down at them. Today, his empty stare felt accusing.

"He didn't call my parents yet," Nella said. "All night, I was so scared."

Carefully, Angela set the toe of one shoe on top of the other. No new shoes for her this year. "What do you mean?"

"I mean, when's he going to? What's he waiting for?"

Angela looked up. Her face was surprised and disappointed. "Don't you know by now?" she said. "I'm no tattletale."

"What?" Gravity let go of Nella. She felt so relieved, it was a miracle she didn't float right up off the pavement. "You didn't tell your father about me?"

"It's not your fault what I did." Angela twisted a braid around her wrist. "And it's not your fault I'm so slow I got caught, either."

"You mean . . . you didn't tell anyone?"

Angela shook her head.

"Even Anthony?"

"I said—"

"I can't believe you did that!" Angela had saved her all over again. Saved her twice. "That was so brave and nice and so . . . Thank you!"

"You'd do it for me," Angela said.

Nella wanted with all her heart for this to be true. She wanted to be just as loyal and brave and good. On the spot she pledged to become the best friend ever born. Never again would Angela get on her nerves! From now on, if other girls were mean to her, Nella would speak right up. She'd order them to stop. She'd make up for everything. She'd be like a saint, the Patron Saint of Secret Sisters.

Victoria and Kimmy came running up, breathless. "My aunt saw the cops bring you home yesterday!" said Kimmy.

Nella's first test of loyalty! She stepped in front of Angela, shielding her.

"I'm sorry to tell you, Kimmy, but your aunt needs an eye transplant."

They ignored her. "What'd you do, Angela? Rob a bank?"

Angela lifted her chin. "Your aunt's right," she said.

Nella couldn't believe it. Was Angela insane? Was she suicidal?

"I got lost. I was trying to find this new, cool store on the west side, but I took the wrong bus, and I didn't know how to get home." She was talking too fast. She was not a good liar. "So I asked a policeman, and he drove me home."

Victoria and Kimmy traded looks.

"Cool store? What *cool store*?"

Angela hesitated.

"When you remember the name of the *cool store*, tell us. We want to be *cool* too, right, Kimmy?"

Nella and Angela watched them stumble away, giggling.

"Where's your lunch?" Angela asked all of a sudden.

"Oh great. I forgot it."

"This is a problem with you," Angela said, smiling faintly.

I'll share was on the tip of Angela's tongue—Nella could almost see the words—when something made them turn around. A space had opened on the playground, and strolling through it was a girl with wiry arms and legs and square black glasses. Her parents walked on either side of

129

her, and they didn't look like any other St. Amphibalus parents. Her father wore a bow tie. Her mother had black hair with a dramatic white streak. Something the father said made the new girl grin. Her smile was electric. It gave Nella a strange, happy jolt.

"Who's she?" said Angela.

What the Statue of
Jeptha A. Stone
Would Say if It Could

Time creeps.
   Time sprints.
Time leaps.
Time stumbles.
My bird—rather, *the* bird—has flown away.
Now and then, time stands still.

BELL AND REM, TIME SISTERS
now

Clem and her parents were about to leave for Cape Cod. The vacation was one step above a death sentence, according to Clem. The water was shark infested and the rays of the sun were lethal. Her parents' friends would descend in droves. They'd eat lobster—which by the way you cooked *live*—and drink wine and ask her repetitive questions. Worst of all, she and Nella wouldn't see each other for weeks.

The night before they left, she gave Nella a crash course in caring for Mr. T.

"Above all," Clem said, "Gentle and Decisive."

"GAD. Got it."

Mrs. Patchett sailed in, bearing a pile of T-shirts she'd bought Clem. They were new but looked old, the misty, blue-green-amber colors of sea glass. In short, perfect for Clem. Who, spoiled-rotten only child that she was, tossed them on her bed without a second look.

Casually, no big deal, Mrs. Patchett gave Nella a key to the house. And a hundred-dollar bill. And profuse thanks, when Nella hadn't even done anything yet. Nella squeaked a thank-you.

"Anybody seen my iPad?" Clem darted out of the bedroom.

While she was gone, Nella lay on the floor and looked up at the glow-in-the-dark galaxy on the ceiling. Turning her head, she noticed a drawing pad under the bed. Inside were sketches for what looked like a comic. "The Adventures of Bell and Rem, Time Sisters."

> *Bell was beautiful, and Rem was a genius. No one could tell who was the hero and who was the sidekick.*
>
> *Bell and Rem possessed magic sabers that could vaporize trash and atomize phonies. But their special power was controlling time. They could make it run faster or slower or stop it altogether, and needless to say this came in very handy when battling the forces of evil.*

Nella flipped the page. Rem and Bell were at St. Ambidextrous School, where they were forced to assume ordinary identities.

> *Bell: I know we're superheroes. But sometimes I wish we were cool and popular, too.*
> *Rem: Are you by any chance implying I'm not cool?*
> *Bell: You know what I mean!*
> *Rem: You are cool. And someday you'll be popular. You've got what it takes. But I'm doomed to life as a weird gerd-neek.*
> *Bell: But I thought you liked being that way.*
> *Rem: Even superheroes can't have everything.*

Across the bottom of the page, Clem had written: *What do we get to choose? And what chooses us? Another mystery of the universe.*

Nella heard Clem coming. Quickly she shoved the comic under the bed and sat up. Clem burst in, waving her iPad. When she flopped onto the rug, her bittersweet citrus smell skewered Nella.

"Approximately 3,025,000 seconds till I'm back."

"Why don't you just say *forever?*"

SEIZE THE DOUGHNUT
then

Clementine Patchett. St. Amphibalus had never seen the like.

She'd moved here from New York City, where she lived in something called the Village. Before that, she'd lived on a houseboat in Amsterdam. For lunch she brought fish tacos or something foul called kimchi, and apparently she had a hedgehog for a pet. She rode a boy's banana bike, and over her uniform wore floppy flannel shirts from the thrift shop. One day during science, when Mrs. Johnson was explaining about the solar system, as if they hadn't been learning about the solar system their entire school lives,

Clem raised her hand. In a helpful voice she said maybe our solar system wasn't the thing to focus on, considering the big picture. Considering it was just an infinitesimal part of a single galaxy. Among countless galaxies. All of which were drifting apart even as they sat here.

Mrs. Johnson tapped the board, but there was no stopping Clem.

"It's just unbelievably cool. The universe is constantly expanding." Clem held up her hands and slowly moved them farther and farther apart. "Think of blueberries spreading in a pancake on a griddle. A griddle without any edges."

"Wait!" Kimmy said, alarmed. "When's that going to stop?"

"Umm, never?"

Not exactly a comforting thought, yet thrilling, in a cold-water-in-the-face way. Watching the new girl with her goofy bandanna and electric smile, her thick glasses and spiky hair, Nella felt like she was waking up. It was like she'd been waiting for this to happen.

After they got over their initial curiosity, the other kids steered clear of Clem. She was so strange, and someone said she wasn't even a Catholic. Victoria subjected her to the usual eye rolling and head shaking, but Clem acted like she didn't even notice.

Meanwhile, Nella labored at being Angela's loyal, true

friend. Since the day she rode home in a police car, Mr. DeMarco had clamped down even harder, which should have been impossible but wasn't. The only places he allowed her to go were church, school, and Nella's house, and that was only because Anthony convinced him Nella was trustworthy and good. They did homework together, and Nella did Angela's nails, even though she had to take the polish off again before she went home. Angela played video games with the boys. She was a butterfingered bumbler, which made them love her all the more passionately. For weeks she staggered around, bent over Vinny as he gripped her fingers. His first, mini-Frankenstein steps were from Mom's arms into Angela's.

"I was afraid you and Angela were growing apart," Mom told Nella. "But you're like sisters, aren't you?"

Anthony got a job at a warehouse on the west side. The company made him cut his hair and wear a black shirt. He worked all night and slept the day away. Angela said she had a vampire for a brother. Nella never saw him now, and she was glad.

I won't tell. How many times had she and Angela promised each other that, doing their secret, four-pinkie swear? Nella kept remembering the face Angela put on for the scowling man in Value Variety: blank, impossible to read. Statue smooth. *Do whatever you want,* said that face.

Don't think you can scare me.

She'd been faking, Nella knew. Beneath that outer calm, her heart had to be pounding like a drum.

What if everyone was faking some way or other?

One day Clem came to school with three dozen Franny's doughnuts. It was her birthday. Mrs. Johnson was not pleased. She tapped her foot, frowning at the big white boxes. The Aroma of Doughnuts made them all shamelessly drool. In the silence, they heard Mrs. Johnson's stomach growl.

"Nella," she said at last, "please help Clementine distribute the doughnuts. One each—don't even start, Samuel!"

"What just happened?" Clem whispered to Nella.

"We're not allowed to have junk food. Only healthy treats."

"Really? That's how it was in New York, but I thought things here were more, you know."

"Ignorant? Primitive?"

"Something like that."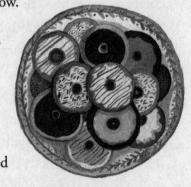
Clem grinned. "Anyway, seize
the day!"

"Seize the doughnut!"

Clem laughed. At lunch-
time, Mrs. Johnson relented

and let them each take a second doughnut. For the first time, Clem sat with Nella and Angela.

"They really are the best doughnuts ever." She put hers on her finger and nibbled. "Physicists speculate the universe is doughnut shaped. Torus, it's called. Umm-umm." She nibbled. "The universe is so delicious."

After that, she ate lunch with them every day. She began walking home with them, on days she didn't have saxophone or karate or astronomy class at the museum. And then one day she invited them to her house. The moment Nella stepped inside, she left behind the neighborhood where she'd lived her whole life. A planet that slipped its orbit and spun loose in the galaxy would feel the way she did then.

Angela was forbidden to go to Clem's house, of course.

"My father doesn't know your parents," she said.

"My mother will call him up!" Clem said. "He can come over and meet them."

"Oh boy," said Angela. "That really won't work."

Clem didn't get it. Apparently she'd never met anyone, even a grown-up, who couldn't be reasoned with.

"Is her father a head case or something?" Clem asked Nella.

"Something."

"He should see a shrink. He should get on meds."

Nella knew she ought to explain about him being a war veteran, and how they needed to respect and honor him, no matter what. But she didn't want to talk about Mr. DeMarco. She was so tired of Mr. DeMarco and all the DeMarco problems. She'd never realized how tired till she met Clem.

Nella promised herself that tomorrow she'd walk home with Angela, same as always. She told herself the same thing the next day, and the next. Every time, Clem invited Angela too. She even got her mother to call up Mr. DeMarco.

"Papa said she's a big honking snob," Angela told Nella.

"She's not. She's nice."

"He said she uses all fifty-cent words." Angela twined her braid around her wrist. "You love vocabulary, so no wonder you like her."

"Who cares about her parents anyway? Half the time they aren't even there."

"That figures. Papa says the people in those town houses only care about money."

"It's not that they don't care about Clem. They trust her, that's all."

A pause.

"Anyway, I don't even want to go."

Angela wasn't allowed to go anywhere but Nella's. Was that Nella's fault?

Sort of. A little.

All Clem knew was what Nella told her. Which did not include having a father who'd been in jail. Or being an escaped shoplifter. Or once planning to marry Anthony and have six daughters whose names all began with *M*. With Clem, Nella erased her old, tarnished self. She drew a shining new girl.

One afternoon that spring, while Nella was helping plant flowers in front of St. A's statue, Sister Rosa said how glad she was Nella had befriended their new student.

"Umm," said Nella.

Sister pulled on her polka-dot garden gloves. She picked up her trowel.

"Make new friends, but keep the old," she said in her honey-and-cream voice. "One is silver and the other's gold."

It's not my fault, Nella wanted to tell her. Angela's not allowed to do anything, but I am. It's just how it is! I'm not choosing, not really. Unless you can choose without choosing.

As they worked, Sister told Nella how years and years and years ago, a parishioner had carved the statue and donated it to the school.

"He wasn't the most skilled craftsman, I'm afraid." She patted the dirt with a polka-dot glove. "But I like to think St. Amphibalus would still be pleased. After all, most saints aren't known for their good looks."

Helping Sister back to her feet, Nella hoped she'd forgotten about Angela and Clem. Sister pulled off the garden gloves one finger at a time, smiling.

"You know the story, don't you? Amphibalus had a very good friend named Alban. When Roman soldiers came to seize Amphibalus, Alban put on his clothes and pretended to be him. They arrested Alban and put him to death. Amphibalus lived to continue his good works. But I bet he had a broken heart the rest of his life."

"What about Alban?"

"Oh, he became a saint too, of course."

Nella brought the hose, and they watered the flowers.

"It's not easy being a saint," Sister said. "Mercy! None of this is easy, Nella. *Follow your own heart!* People always say that. They mean well, I'm sure. But sometimes, we need to overrule our hearts. We need to be brave. We need to be kind because we should, not because it's easy."

"Isn't that being fake?" Nella blurted.

"Kindness is the truest thing there is."

Nuns were not plagued by questions. They never had doubts or got confused. So what Sister said next was a surprise.

"Sometimes I'm glad I'm old." She took Nella's arm. "Being young is so much work."

BUONA FESTA!
now

"The bishop kisses up to the suburbs. The big houses and fat wallets." Mr. Tucci, Victoria's uncle, pinched his thumb and forefinger together. "The dollar sign—that's what matters."

The other men outside the smoke shop nodded and grunted. Mr. DeMarco wasn't there today. Come to think of it, Nella hadn't seen him there in a long time. She struggled to push the stroller past the men, but the thing had taken so much abuse, its front wheels were out of whack. From behind her came the racket of hammers and drills—they were already gutting the school. A sign outside said

FUTURE HOME OF THE HEAVENLY SPA.

"He's got the church in his sights next," Mr. Tucci said. "Wait and see."

"Over my dead body!" said another man. "Four generations of my family got christened, married, and buried out of St. A."

"Problem is," said someone else, "nowadays we got way more funerals than baptisms."

"Hey. Hey, whose side you on?"

"We built this place!" Mr. Tucci jabbed the air with his cigar. "Our families built it with their own hands. Now we're just doormats. They're wiping their designer shoes on us."

"I'll tell you this. My grandfather's turning over in his grave about what's happening here. Back in the sixties, he defended his home. No way he was going to let outsiders come in and . . ." The man spat on the sidewalk.

"You're a bunch of hotheads. You're living in the past."

"The past was better. Turn back the clock."

That was when Mr. Tucci noticed Nella spinning her wheels. He jumped up to help.

"How's your nonni?" His cigar breath almost asphyxiated her.

"She's okay." And then out came the phrase Nonni always used. *"Così così."* So-so. *Whatever.*

144

Mr. Tucci maneuvered the stroller around the sidewalk chairs.

"Nobody made sauce like hers, you know that?" He smiled. "The other ladies begged for her recipe, but no way she'd give it to them. I remember her and your poppop dancing at my wedding. Heck, the whole neighborhood danced at my wedding, but your nonni outlasted them all."

Nonni dancing the night away? Cigar smoke must have damaged the man's brain.

"Boocha!" cried Vinny, pointing at the sky. "Boocha ganna!"

Mr. Tucci gave him a funny look. "Can't that kid talk yet?" Putting his face close to Vinny's, he spoke slowly and much too loudly. "Say airplane. Air-plane."

Vinny put one hand over his eyes and the other over his nose. "Nabba," he said. Which clearly meant *Please go away, smelly man*.

A few days later was the Feast. Once it had been a mostly neighborhood affair, with a Mass in honor of St. A and a block party afterward.

But over the years it had gotten bigger and bigger, till now people came from all over the city and suburbs. For days before, the church kitchen went 24-7, women in hairnets rolling out miles of pasta and stirring gallons of tomato sauce with big paddles. They made thousands of meatballs. Everyone prayed to St. Amphibalus for good weather, no rain.

He listened. That night, after Mass, and the procession with the little brass band, and the recent First Communicants riding on the back of a truck, and the Knights of Columbus marching in their sashes and white gloves, the street filled with people. The grills and fryers fired up, and you could practically eat the air. Sausage and peppers, cavatelli and meatballs, stromboli and gelato. Carnival rides and games in the church parking lot, gambling in the basement, drinking and dancing in a fenced-off square behind Mama Gemma's.

Nella helped Dad work the sausage-and-peppers stand. When he threw the links on the grill, clouds of smoke rose. Sweat trickled down the sides of his face, and his apron was streaked with grease. He clicked the big tongs like castanets, making her smile.

It was almost like before, when he was still her old, trustworthy dad. They worked side by side without talking much, a team, together.

Customers piled up three and four deep. If Clem had been here, Nella would have asked what law of physics explained how so many people could cram into such a small space. Nella got hugs from aunts and cousins who lived out in the boonies now. Two ugly ducklings who thought they were swans glided by—wait, no. It was Victoria and Kimmy. Nella wiped her brow. It was so hot near the grill, her hair was sweat-glued to her forehead. She was sure the pimples on her chin were swelling in the slippery heat.

"What's it take to get service around this place?" Mr. Ferraro bellowed. Beside him stood his wife and oh no. Please no. Sam. Her face was already so sweaty, blushing was beside the point.

"Look who's cooking, hon! Is our life insurance paid up?"

Mr. Ferraro was known for being a joker. When Nella was little, she was scared of him, he talked so loud. Sam smiled at Nella and shrugged. She clamped her arms to her sides in a pathetic attempt to conceal her pit sweat.

"Give me three of those babies, Nick, and throw in some Cokes."

Dad tucked the sausages into rolls, and Nella added the peppers and onions. Mr. Ferraro handed over the money, and Dad made the change. But as he took it, Mr. Ferraro's smile vanished.

"Hey, big mistake here." A human megaphone. "I gave you two twenties!"

"Sorry, Bill. It was a twenty and a ten."

"Hold on. Hold on a gosh-darn, flat-out, Christian minute." Mr. Ferraro slapped his pocket like somebody was trying to pick it. "I don't make mistakes when it comes to money!"

Nella could see the ten-dollar bill, lying right on top in the cash box. The other customers grew quiet, tuning in to the drama.

"Looks like it comes down to my word against yours!" Mr. Ferraro's voice took on a hint of menace.

A long pause. Slowly, Dad pulled out some bills.

"The customer's always right."

Mr. Ferraro's face shone with satisfaction. Nella looked to see what Sam would do, but he had vanished.

"Never mind, Nick." Mr. Ferraro smiled a wide, ugly FART of a smile. "Everybody makes a mistake now and then. Am I right? Am I right? Consider it a donation to the church." He took his wife's arm. "Come on, hon."

Dad quietly clicked his tongs. Open shut, open shut. Then he wiped his brow with his apron and asked the next customer what he could do for him.

Later, Nella stood behind the church, where the rides and games were set up. Bobby and his friend screamed their heads off on the Tilt-A-Whirl. Salvatore won a blow-up baseball bat at the ring toss game and, to Nella's astonishment, handed it to a girl with sparkly butterfly barrettes.

She peeked into the church basement. No kids allowed.

Mom didn't approve of gambling, but Dad said it was the church's biggest moneymaker so what could you do. Nella saw men's hunched backs, heard someone shout and someone groan. She jumped back as a couple of men, looking unhappy, muttering to each other, came up the steps. Moments later, a few more men trudged up, trailing something—anger, frustration—behind them and out into the night.

Nella squeezed sideways through the crowds. She could smell herself—a walking sausage. The lines were long, and once you got your food there was no room to eat it. People jostled and elbowed, and a plate of meatballs launched skyward and splatted onto the street. A little girl dropped her elephant ear and it was immediately trampled. Babies cried. Some guys who stank like they had taken a bath in beer staggered through, laughing, spouting four-letter words.

Invaders, thought Nella. Overhead, the moon looked farther away than usual.

She saw Sam, standing alone, one foot propped against the wall of the social club. Wheeling in the opposite direction, she pushed deeper into the crowd. By the time she made her way to the lit-up bocce court, she was tired and cranky.

"*Buona festa*, Nella!" Mrs. Manzini called. Her little

daughter, dragging her blankie, did an echo. "*Buona festa*, Nella!"

Nella said it back, but this party didn't feel happy to her. The bocce players, who always took the game seriously, looked irritable, even more ready to argue than usual. They had the tape measure out, measuring the distance between balls, and everyone was leaning forward, gesturing, offering an opinion.

A bunch of college kids sat on the wall, spooning up gelato. They didn't know the first thing about bocce. They looked amused, like they were observing zoo animals doing something weird.

Nella's bad mood got worse.

It was dark now, almost time for the fireworks. Never, ever had Nella missed the fireworks, which she loved. She started back toward the playground, where her family always sat to watch. She'd cuddle Vinny on her lap, put her hands over his ears. *Fireworks,* she'd tell him, pronouncing the word slowly and distinctly, the way the pediatrician said they should. *Gold. Red. Blue.*

Was she imagining it, or were there more police here than earlier? She passed one holding a crackling radio. Feeling uneasy, longing for her family, she tried to move faster, but it was gridlock. *Whomp!* The first firework rose and exploded. All around her people craned their necks, and their faces took on an eerie, red-tinged glow.

Whomp! Whomp! Nella was trapped. The thick air took on that smell that always made her think of guns and war. The explosions rattled her chest. Hazy smoke rose in the streetlights. Across the street, at the bocce courts, voices began to shout. Nella couldn't see what was happening, and at first she thought it was just the players having an especially loud argument, but now police officers muscled their way through the crowd.

"Coming through, coming through."

Whomp! Whomp! A girl screamed.

"A fight," somebody said. "Those damn college kids."

People pushed one another, trying to see. Jostling, shoving. The air itself felt explosive, and Nella wanted only one thing. To be with her family.

Now, another wave of people shoved her backward up the hill, and she stumbled over the curb and onto the sidewalk. In front of Franny's, where a SOLD OUT sign was taped to the window, a lunatic pigeon dodged among all the feet. Peering through the crowd, Nella saw a familiar gleam of yellow hair. Angela? But who was she with? An old man who shaded his eyes as if caught in a blinding glare. Like Nella, they were trying to make their way down the hill, away from this. The old man was stooped almost in half, and Angela's arm was tight around him, like she was all that held him together. Like without her, he'd fly into pieces.

Another firework was launched, and as it burst Nella realized—the man was Angela's father. That old, sick man was Mr. DeMarco. Red rocket light fell across his face, and on it Nella saw her own fear. Times a thousand.

Where was Anthony? Instinctively, she looked around. Something bad was happening—they needed Anthony!

But then she remembered: Anthony worked at night now.

The hungry mouth of the crowd swallowed them down. Trembling, on the verge of tears, Nella pushed her way forward till she finally reached the playground. There they were, in the same place they sat every year: her parents in their lawn chairs and the boys on the pony blanket at their feet. Nella grabbed Vinny and squeezed him tight.

"Nella." Her mother took her hand. "Where were you? Are you all right?"

Now I am.

It was a fight between neighborhood boys and outsiders, they heard the next day. Kenny Lombardo was hitting on a college girl and wouldn't take no for an answer. Or a college guy taunted Kenny, calling him a goombah and worse. Or some thugs from the bottom of the hill showed up, just looking for trouble. Friends got involved. Bystanders got involved. Punches got thrown. A nose got broken. Arrests were made.

"Something wasn't right this year," said Mom. "There was a bad feeling in the air. I'm glad it's over, and things can get back to normal."

But the street was a disaster: trash everywhere, bushes broken and flower beds crushed, like an invading army had marched through. The bad feeling was still in the air. *Over* didn't feel like the right word.

What the Statue of Jeptha A. Stone Would Say if It Could

The bird having left is, need I say, a great relief.
   An enormous relief.
A colossal relief.
That foolishness is *over*.
I can once more resume my monumental dignity.
Hark unto me, Jeptha A. Stone: I do not miss her.
(How could I, with a heart made of stone?)

TOO LATE
now

Tonight Nella had two duties, one pleasant, one a drag. She chose pleasant first.

She let herself into Clem's house, where the Patchetts had left the AC on low, so Mr. T wouldn't suffer in the heat. Nella's heart lifted when she saw him, a sign of just how pathetically lonesome she was. Gentle and Decisive, she worked on winning his confidence. For the first time, when she slid her hand toward him he didn't do his crazy huffing and puffing. Nella told him what a brilliant hedgehog he was, then gently and decisively put him back.

She opened the drawers of Clem's dresser. She'd already checked under the bed, and in the closet, but "The Adventures of Bell and Rem" was nowhere to be found. Nella knew she shouldn't snoop, but she needed to know what happened to those two.

She watered Mrs. Patchett's patio tomatoes and pinched off the suckers, the way Nonni had taught her. Back inside, cool, silky air washing over her, she fetched a mango-flavored sparkling water from the fridge and lay on the hands-down-most-comfortable couch in the world. She flipped on the TV and watched in exquisite, brotherless peace. When she grew up, she'd have a place just like this. Only in a different city. Chicago, maybe, or New York. Maybe she and Clem would share an apartment. She stretched her legs, and maybe they weren't so ugly. Maybe they were even getting a little shapely, as they said in magazines.

Nella folded her hands beneath her head. Her fingers gave off tomato-plant stink. On TV, film stars in evening gowns, hands on hips, pivoted this way and that in the flashing lights. Nella chose the red dress. No, the silver one. It was so exquisite, like a bell, a bell made of liquid silver, a bell ringing in a tower, a silvery song pealing across the land, *Nella, Bella . . .*

The second she woke up she remembered her other

duty and knew she was in serious trouble. She could feel how late it was even before she looked at the clock. Then realized it was even later.

Nella ran all the way. Nonni would eat her alive. She'd never hear the end of what a lazy, selfish *ragazza* she was.

Nonni's front windows were dark. Nella peered in, but the hall light was off too. This was bad. Nella couldn't even apologize and promise it would never, ever happen again. Nonni would be completely in the right, and Nella would be sentenced to life in the Prison of Criticism.

Across the street, every window glowed with light. Keyboard music floated out. Hairy Boy's bike was locked to a porch spindle.

If only there was no Nonni. If only she'd disappear. Not die, of course, but embark on an endless cruise or train trip.

Music and laughter spilled out the windows across the street. The purple curtains rippled. Over there, everything danced.

Nothing for her to do but go home and get lectured.

She was lucky. Dad had already gone to bed. This summer, the heat, and the lazy-good-for-nothing-college-student summer hires were really taking it out of him, Mom said. She looked pretty tired herself, but she had the sewing machine out, mending the cavemen's ripped shirts and shorts. In her faded jeans, she reminded Nella of Cinderella, only her fairy godmother didn't show up, so she was making her own dress. Nella-Bella-Cinderella, that was another nickname Anthony used to call her. Mom bit off a thread.

"Where have you been?"

Nonni didn't call and rat on her? It was like a tornado not touching down. A miracle.

"Oh, you know," said Nella.

Mom cocked her head, considering. "I guess you're old enough to have a secret or two." She smiled. "Just remember I trust you."

"Good night!" Nella took the stairs two at a time.

Sister Rosa rarely talked about sin. She preferred to emphasize the positive. But Nella remembered the time she taught them the difference between sins of commission and sins of omission.

Such as omitting to tell you neglected your duty.

But when you got away with something, it felt like heaven was smiling down on you. *You get a pass,* heaven whispered.

Besides, Nonni would tell. It was only a matter of time. Time.

Just before she tumbled into sleep, Nella heard sirens. They went on and on. They echoed through her dreams.

THE NEWS
now

All night long, Nonni pestered Nella. She starred in every insane, mixed-up dream, now eating a ripe fig, now dragging a dreadful, inert object down the hallway to the kitchen. Just before Nella woke up for good, Nonni appeared holding a fat white jug. Though Nella tried to stop her, she tilted it and a waterfall of milk poured out. *No!* cried Nella. *No!* But Nonni just shook her head as the last drop drained away. *Too late.*

The words jolted Nella awake. Pulling on her clothes, she hurried up the hill. All traces of the Feast were cleaned up by now, but the air still felt unsettled. Disturbed. It was so early, everything was closed up except for Franny's, where doughnut fragrance made her weak in the knees. *Doughnut is the universal language,* Clem liked to say. *We all speak doughnut.*

Once Nella made sure Nonni was okay, she'd come back and buy a cake doughnut. She'd go home and pour herself a glass of cold milk.

Nonni spilling the milk—the dream broke over her again. And then the memory of standing here watching Angela help her father through the crowd. Like a guardian angel, that's how she'd looked. Up the hill, on the sidewalk, bits of something glinted in the early light. Was it glass? A car accident? Was that why she'd heard the sirens? Uneasiness rippled out around her, like she was a pebble dropped in a pond.

Across the street from Nonni's, the purple curtains hung still and lifeless.

Nonni wouldn't answer the door. It wasn't locked, a surprise, since Nonni was on perpetual guard against Gypsy thieves. The air in the front hall was a thick soup nobody had stirred for a long time. In the kitchen Nonni sat in her worse-for-wear nightgown, hands folded on the fake lace tablecloth.

"Ciao," said Nella, but Nonni didn't turn around. The little TV, tuned to a news station, was up loud.

"The critically wounded twenty-two-year-old was a star high school football player," said a reporter whose lipstick matched her bright-red suit. "According to his family, he is the father of two young boys."

"Nonni? Hi, Nonni!"

At last, her great-grandmother noticed her. She started to raise a hand, but it drifted back down. What was that on her chin?

"Terror!" she seemed to say.

Terrorists? Was that what she meant? The TV showed a front yard marked off with police tape. A voice-over said something about early this morning, a young mother home alone with her child. A knock on her door. A man trying to break in. Great! This was Nonni's favorite kind of news story, some terrible tragedy that befell utter strangers. She'd be talking about it all day.

The screen flashed to a young, brown-skinned man with a broad smile. Last night's sirens echoed in Nella's head, and she was suddenly cold. She didn't want to hear this. This was no way to start a day!

"I'm just going to turn this down a little." But as she leaned forward, the screen split in half and a second face appeared. A young, white-skinned man with a stunned look. Something made Nella touch her finger to the screen.

"No no!" moaned Nonni, and Nella quickly drew back, sure she was being scolded. But she couldn't take her eyes from the TV, and a second later she snatched her hand away as if the screen had burned her. Because it was Anthony. It was Anthony DeMarco Jr. who in the early-morning hours shot the handsome, smiling black man.

Two shots, said the reporter with the bloodred mouth and suit to match. One to the arm, the other to the abdomen. In critical condition at University Hospital.

Nella sank into the chair beside Nonni. The TV seemed to grow louder yet, the reporter's grating voice pressing in from all sides. Nella stared at the screen, wondering how they could make such a mistake. That man looked like Anthony, but it couldn't be. Not her Anthony.

Unless. Unless he was protecting someone. The mother in the house alone with her baby. But they didn't seem to be calling him a hero. Crimson Mouth frowned with distaste as she pronounced his name. Nella turned back to Nonni.

"What can they . . ."

But something was wrong. Something else. One of her great-grandmother's eyes was unnaturally wide, while the other was half closed. One side of Nonni's face drooped, like the muscles had given up.

She opened her mouth and nonsense spilled out.

"Nonni! What's wrong?"

A moan, soft as a baby in her sleep. Nonni's arm jutted out, knocking her coffee cup to the floor, where it shattered.

Nella jumped up. She switched off the TV, like that might help. Nonni kept trying to raise her arm, but it flopped on the table like a dying fish. More garbled, urgent sounds. *Stroke.* The word went neon in Nella's brain. It was something Dad and Mom had worried about.

"I'm calling the doctor." She tried to keep her voice calm. "Don't worry, Nonni. It's going to be okay."

Grabbing the phone, dialing 911, telling the dispatcher what was happening, reciting the address. All the while, she watched herself from some misty distance.

"They're coming," she told Nonni, who kept trying and failing to lift her arm. "Stop, Nonni, don't. Just stay still, they're coming."

But now her great-grandmother summoned a superhero's strength, and her good hand plucked at her worn nightgown. Nella understood: she was embarrassed to be seen like this. Nella raced to the bedroom and found the pretty robe they gave her for Christmas. It still had the tags on it, because Nonni said it was too fancy, but now she let Nella wrap it around her bent shoulders, and slide the matching slippers on her bony feet, just in time for the EMS guys who burst through the door.

FLIP BOOK
now

Her brain was a flip book.

Anthony's frightened face on TV.

Nonni slumped against the wall, feet cocked at a sickening angle.

Flashing lights, Nonni strapped to a stretcher, disappearing into the back of an ambulance.

The blank TV.

She couldn't stop the images flashing through her mind.

Mom and Dad were at the hospital, and Nella was in charge of the boys. Vinny and Bobby were parked in front of some idiotic TV show. Vinny's head rested on Bobby's belly. Bobby sucked his thumb and absentmindedly twirled his little brother's silky hair. They were a two-man comfort machine, and Nella yearned to lie down with them. Instead, she washed dishes, folded laundry. Prayed. She was exhausted and electrified at the same time, and her useless brain kept flashing like an appliance on the blink. Holding the phone, she stepped out on the porch. Salvatore and Kevin raced toward the house.

"Is Nonni dead?" cried Kevin, panting.

"No! Don't even say that!"

"Anthony DeMarco shot a guy dead," he said, like being dead was contagious. "He shot him right between the eyes."

"In the stomach," Salvatore corrected. "And he's not dead yet."

"There was blood all over the sidewalk!"

"They washed it off." Salvatore swallowed. "But you can still tell."

"Anthony's in jail," Kevin said. "Angela's crying her head off."

"You saw her?"

"No, but I bet she is."

They looked at her expectantly, waiting for her to tell them it was okay, it would be all right. Nella, who spent half her life wishing they'd vaporize, felt helpless and terrible. She was letting them down.

"It was at Mrs. Manzini's house," said Salvatore.

"What?"

This had to be wrong. Mrs. Manzini? Nella had just seen her at the Feast, her and her little girl dragging the blankie. *Buona festa!* they sang. They were not the kind of people to have a shoot-out in their front yard. Blood on their sidewalk. Her knees went weak.

"The black guy banged on their door," said Salvatore.

How could he know so much more than she did? The phone in Nella's hand rang. She'd forgotten she was even holding it, and a tiny scream flew out of her. Both brothers jumped in fright.

It was their mother's cell.

What if Nonni died? The world faded, all its colors bleaching away. Everything went flimsy, even the massive wall of the cemetery.

The phone kept ringing. As long as Nella didn't answer, Nonni was alive. Her brothers gaped at her.

"Answer!" said Salvatore.

How could she ever have gotten upset over things like being too tall or having too many brothers? How could she ever have wished Nonni would disappear? All the vengeful things she'd done, like pretending she couldn't find

Nonni's remote or favorite black sweater, lying to Ernestina that Nonni couldn't come to the phone when she'd been waiting all day for her friend to call. How could Nella have done that? How could she have been so stupid and selfish?

Salvatore grabbed the phone and hit *talk*. She grabbed it back.

"Nella! At last!"

"Mom!"

"Nonni had a stroke. It's serious, but they think she'll pull through. Nella?"

"Oh. Oh!"

"Is Nonni okay?" asked Salvatore.

Nella nodded, and Kevin threw his arms around her middle as if she'd saved Nonni. Crazy love flooded through her. Fierce, feverish, big-sister love. She'd never get mad at them again, no matter what they did. Never, ever would she take people she loved for granted as long as she lived.

"It's so lucky you were there," Mom was saying. "The doctor says quick treatment saved her life. What were you doing there so early? Never mind, tell me later. I'm coming soon. Wait. . . ."

Nella heard her father's voice in the background. Her mother got back on. "Dad says to tell you how proud he is of you, Bella."

Nella croaked something and hung up. Kevin wriggled

away from her, and already her relief started to ebb. The only reason she was there so early this morning was she was too late last night. Why didn't Nonni call Mom and Dad last night when Nella didn't show up? Maybe she was already getting sick, while Nella lounged on Clem's couch, sipping mango fizzy water and dreaming of a silver evening gown.

The cemetery wall once again rose straight and blunt, no longer flimsy. She was not a hero. Saving Nonni was a big fat accident.

A yellow-flecked bird swooped over the cemetery wall and vanished among the trees. Salvatore and Kevin went inside, letting the screen door bang behind them.

Clem's cell phone went straight to her message.

"You've reached me in a galaxy far far away—if only!"

Clem would listen. She'd sympathize and try to help, but she wouldn't understand. She barely knew Nonni. All she knew was that Nonni enjoyed making Nella's life miserable.

Angela. She was the one who'd understand. Angela was practically an honorary great-grandchild.

Now it came rushing back. Anthony. Anthony shot someone.

Inside, Vinny was crying. Nella wiped his runny nose, fed him lunch, read to him till he fell asleep. When Mom finally got home, she was a wreck. Nonni couldn't talk. Her left side was useless. She was too fragile for surgery and it was too soon to say if she'd recover.

"How much, I mean," Mom corrected herself. "Not if."

Was that supposed to be a smile? Mom was a relentless optimist, so seeing her this upset was scary. Vinny staggered into the room, rubbing his eyes, and Mom cuddled him.

"Why did the stroke happen?" Afraid as she was of the answer, Nella had to ask.

"We don't know. She takes medication for her high blood pressure." Mom's voice broke, and Vinny patted her cheek, murmuring incomprehensible comfort. "The doctor said sometimes an emotional upset can trigger a stroke, but that can't be. Nonni's always upset!"

Mom said they needed to wait till the swelling in the brain went down before they knew more. Nella imagined a brain inflating like a pink blister. She pressed her hands to the sides of her head as if it was hers.

What the Statue of
Jeptha A. Stone
Would Say if It Could

This afternoon, I could scarcely credit the evidence of my own expertly carved eyeballs.

Singing merrily, winging her way back to me.

Huzzah! Hooray!

Ahem.

I mean, *Alas! Alack!*

ANGELA DEMARCO HAS
NO FRIENDS
now

They used the same two photos over and over.

One: D'Lon Andrews, wearing a confident smile.

Two: Anthony, looking like he was gripped by a nightmare and couldn't wake up.

Nella read the newspaper account so many times she could almost recite it.

UNARMED MAN SHOT IN LITTLE ITALY

Early Thursday morning, an off-duty security guard shot an unarmed man in the neighborhood known as Little Italy. D'Lon Andrews, 22, was seeking help following a car accident when he was shot, police officials said. He remains in critical condition at University Hospital.

According to authorities, Anthony DeMarco Jr., 19, fired twice, striking the victim in the arm and abdomen.

Andrews, who lives in the Garfield neighborhood, had spent the night with friends. While Andrews was driving home, his car went off the road and hit the massive wall of Hilltop Cemetery. Andrews proceeded down the hill seeking help. He knocked on several doors, none of which opened.

Elaine Manzini, 30, heard knocking shortly after midnight. Thinking it was her husband, who was at work, she opened the door. When she saw Andrews, whose face was bloody, she panicked and called 911. She reported a man trying to break into the house, where she was alone with her child.

DeMarco, on his way home from his shift as a guard for Vigilant Security, arrived on the scene. Hearing screams from inside the house, he ordered the man to halt. Instead, Andrews ran toward him.

Nella had to pause when she got to this part. She saw Anthony all alone, a stranger rushing toward him in the dark. She heard the screaming.

> According to DeMarco's account, he ordered
> Andrews to put his hands up. Andrews continued to
> yell incomprehensibly and to come toward him. He
> reached inside his jacket. DeMarco opened fire.
>
> Police arrived as DeMarco was performing CPR
> on the victim. Andrews is employed as an aide at
> Stone Gardens Nursing Home. He is the father of two
> young sons.
>
> Little Italy was the scene of other recent arrests at
> the Feast of St. Amphibalus. A number of residents
> were charged with disturbing the peace, assault, dis-
> orderly conduct, and resisting arrest.

Nella laid the paper down. Inside her, questions crashed
into each other like bumper cars. What was wrong with
D'Lon Andrews? Why didn't he call somebody he knew
instead of knocking on strange doors? Why didn't he stop
when Anthony told him to? What was he yelling, and why
did he reach in his jacket if he didn't have a gun?

The last time she'd seen Anthony was that afternoon
at Nonni's house. She remembered his dark uniform
and close-clipped hair. The belt he wore, with all those
unfriendly things attached to it. He looked like he was

wearing a costume, like an actor cast in a role he didn't want.

And he was angry. Anthony, always so scrawny, had muscles, coiled tight under his skin. Ready to jump and strike.

Nella pushed that memory away. Far away.

Dear God, please make D'Lon Andrews get better. Please don't let Nonni die. Please shower Your loving mercy upon them both. And on those who love them.

At noon, she and Mom watched the news. Mr. Andrews's fiancée, a slender woman with eyes swollen to slits, attempted to make a statement. She stood outside the house where she lived with their two little boys, a small house with a crooked metal awning. It looked a lot like the houses here in Little Italy.

"D'Lon is a loving son, a loving fiancé, and a loving father." Her eyes filled with new tears. "We are all praying . . . praying to God . . ."

Her voice broke. Another woman put an arm around her and took her inside.

They played the 911 tape of Mrs. Manzini. She yelled that a black man covered in blood was trying to break into her house. Her little girl screamed in the background. Mrs. Manzini sobbed, she was alone, please hurry, hurry.

"Someone else is here," she said then. "Oh my God! He

has a gun!" The tape broke off.

The reporter, today wearing a turquoise suit, repeated: "Andrews was unarmed. Toxicology reports are incomplete. *Channel 6 News* will continue to closely follow this tragic event."

Mom grabbed a sponge and scrubbed the same spot on the counter over and over.

"I can't understand it," she said. "Anthony of all people!"

"What do you mean?" Nella saw him in that uniform—angry and tense and miserable. "It's not his fault! He thought the guy had a gun!"

Way too much time went by before Mom spoke.

"That poor, sweet boy."

Which boy did she mean?

"One mistake." Mom scrubbed and scrubbed. "That's all it takes." All of a sudden she stopped and turned to Nella. "What about Angela? Did you call her?"

"Mom." Nella looked away. "We're not really friends anymore."

"Don't be silly! Of course you are."

Mom didn't like complicated. She preferred simple, a philosophy that worked fine with snot-nosed little boys.

The TV, showing some kids at a cooking camp, suddenly cut away. Breaking news.

"We have just received word from doctors at University Hospital that D'Lon Andrews, unarmed victim of a shooting in Little Italy, has died of a gunshot wound."

Time stopped.

The reporter said it again, as if she knew Nella wouldn't believe it the first time.

"We have just received word . . ."

"Oh no," whispered Mom. She clutched the wet sponge to her chest, where it made a dark spot. "Not again."

Dad. Somehow Nella knew her mother was remembering what had happened to him. The past rushed up and plowed into the present, a terrible collision, a horrible accident.

The TV cut to someone—who was it? Some man, a friend or relative of D'Lon Andrews.

"D'Lon's the guy always helping others. He's there for you, man, no matter what." He was so angry, he could hardly choke the words out. "When he got hurt he went looking for help. He thought he'd get treated the way he treated any living creature—animal, human, no matter." He dug the heel of his palm into his eyes. "Instead, he got shot. He trusted other people and he got a bullet."

"No," whispered Nella. This was wrong. Time, stopped in its tracks, lurched forward again. The wrongness of what the man just said made the world start back up. Anthony wouldn't hurt a fly. He was trying to help, not hurt. Nella knew it.

She *knew* it.

"Where are you going?" asked Mom as Nella pulled a cap over her messy hair.

"To see Angela."

"Take Vinny. You know how she loves him."

Nella grabbed her brother. The stupid stroller kept trying to veer left, and it took all her determination to forge ahead.

Outside the smoke shop, the conversation was loud and intense.

"That boy had to be drunk out of his mind. Banging on doors in the middle of the night?"

"Maybe he had a concussion? Didn't know where he was."

"It was midnight! He drove off the road! Why wasn't he home with his wife and kids?"

"*Girlfriend* and kids."

"Some stranger threatens me and my family, I'm ready. That's all I got to say. I am armed and ready."

"Anthony Jr.? That kid always looked scared of his own shadow."

The men flicked cigar ashes onto the sidewalk. Their eyes slid to Mr. DeMarco's empty chair. Today, nobody paid any attention to Nella.

A woman at the bus stop was reading the paper, and Nella glimpsed Anthony's face, creased and wrinkled. Vinny banged his heels against the stroller and leaned forward, like a ship's captain ordering full speed ahead.

But when they got to Angela's block, Nella skidded to a halt. TV vans blocked the narrow street. Strangers with cameras and headsets clustered outside the DeMarco house. At the foot of the front steps, arms folded across his chest, a burly police officer stood guard. People from the neighborhood clustered and watched.

"Nella!" Sam waved. He was with Victoria and Kimmy. Nella manhandled the stroller around a van parked right up on the sidewalk and almost clipped a woman in a turquoise suit. The TV reporter! She was picking her teeth in the side-view mirror. People on TV never seemed real. Not real real. But something slimy and disgusting was stuck between the woman's very real front teeth.

"Oh my God, oh my God!" Victoria grabbed Nella's arm. She was out of breath. "Can you believe this?" She wore mascara and a cute shirt, like she was on her way to a party. "I already got interviewed by a blogger."

"The story's going viral, now that the guy died," said Kimmy.

Nella looked at Angela's house. A faded American flag

hung from a pole. All the curtains were pulled tight.

"Viral!" she said. "Why?"

"The guy is black and Anthony's white." Victoria gave her hair an impatient flip. "It's like, you know. Civil rights. People are totally outraged. The blogger dude said it's already trending."

"What?" repeated Nella, and Victoria rolled her eyes so high in her head, it was amazing they didn't get stuck up there.

Sam scowled and punched the air. Nella hadn't seen him since that awful night at the sausage stand. She looked even worse today, sweaty from pushing the stupid stroller, her hair a disaster.

"I'm on Anthony's side," he was saying. "But—"

"But what?" Victoria's hands flew to her hips. "Mrs. Manzini was all alone with her baby! What do you expect her to do, open the door to a guy covered in blood and say, *Can I help you? Would you like a cup of tea?*"

"I would've died of fright," put in Kimmy.

"Are you saying the guy deserved to get shot?" asked Sam.

"Nobody *deserves* to get shot, Samuel Ferraro." Victoria lifted her chin. "But sometimes there are *circumstances*."

"Maybe it was no one's fault," said Nella.

"Oh my God!" Victoria threw her hands in the air.

"Like any judge is going to say that."

The judge. Nella hadn't thought ahead to all that. The sun beat down. The sidewalk sizzled. Vinny was fussing, and Nella lifted him from the stroller. Grabbing her T-shirt, he scrubbed his boogery nose against it before she could stop him.

"I heard about your great-grandmother," Sam said then. "Is she okay?"

"We don't know for sure yet. We have to wait and see."

"That stinks. That's messed up." He actually sounded like he cared. "Man! What is up with this neighborhood?"

Nella stared at Angela's house and tried to remember before, but the past was gone, stolen clean away. Time was a thief. It was lawless. Time should go to jail. Vinny kicked her, wanting to be set down, but she needed something solid to hold on to, even if it was a snotty, squirmy brother.

A sudden commotion broke out. The DeMarco front door was opening, and the crowd of media surged forward. The police officer set his legs far apart and spread his arms, a human barricade.

"Do not cross this line!"

Mr. DeMarco stepped outside. He looked terrible. He had dark rings under his eyes. His white T-shirt barely covered his sagging belly, and his arms were so hairy, all that matted yellow hair. Nella strained to see behind him, but the doorway was dark.

The media people all shouted questions at the same time. Nella saw the house the way it would look on the news. The drawn curtains. The limp flag. No shrubs or bushes, just those cracked concrete steps. Mr. DeMarco blinked and looked confused, as if he wasn't sure what was happening. He raised a hand, like a person under attack.

"What was your reaction when you heard what your son did?" someone shouted.

"Does he have a history of violence?"

Mr. DeMarco swayed. He caught at the railing. From the corner of her eye, Nella saw the living-room curtains move. A pale oval floated behind the glass. Nella's arms tightened around Vinny.

"Do you know where he obtained the gun?"

"Is it true your wife abandoned the family?"

The face behind the glass seemed to flicker in and out.

"Has your son expressed regret for his actions?"

Mr. DeMarco drew himself up.

"My son is a brave boy! He was doing his duty. If you can't understand that, you can go straight to hell." He stumbled back over the threshold. "Now go away and leave us alone!" The door slammed. The living-room curtain fell back into place.

"Oh. My. God," breathed Victoria.

"He's so gross and terrifying," said Kimmy. "No wonder Angela's the way she is."

"Here they come!" squealed Victoria. She patted her hair and smoothed her shirt as the reporter in the turquoise suit marched across the street. A red-haired young guy with a camera on his shoulder trudged behind.

Some neighbors shielded their faces, refusing to comment, but others were eager to say what a good, quiet boy Anthony Jr. was. He was at church every Sunday. Since their mother left, he was even more devoted to his little sister. *Was was was*, like he was the one who'd died.

Vinny sneezed translucent green bubbles just as Turquoise Suit and the cameraman approached. With a disgusted face, the reporter pivoted away and held the mic out to Victoria.

Who was ready. Who was born for this moment. Her face went beatific as a saint in a holy painting. She said she went to school with Anthony's little sister. Angela was nice, Victoria said, but personally, she felt extremely sorry for her.

"Sorry?" The reporter went on high alert. "How so?"

"Her father's totally strict. He has a really wicked temper, like you just saw." Victoria's ultra-lashes fluttered. "Her mother had a nervous breakdown, so all Angela's got is her brother. She doesn't really have any friends."

The red-haired man peeked out from behind his camera, his face sad. Not Turquoise Suit. She ate this up. She got Victoria's name, then dashed back to her van, gesturing to the camera guy to hurry up.

"Oh my God," said Victoria. "I sounded like a complete loser!"

Sam and Kimmy assured her she didn't, but Nella couldn't even look at her. Why? It wasn't as if Victoria had lied. Mr. DeMarco was as bad as she said. Mrs. DeMarco did run away. And the part about Angela not having any real friends? Well.

Nella tried to put Vinny back in the stroller, but he arched his back and spouted his embarrassing gibberish. He yanked the cap off her head and threw it in the filthy gutter. Her messy hair fell in her face. If so many people weren't around, she might have smacked him.

"This is unreal," Sam said. "It's like we're in a movie. We're part of somebody's script."

"And exactly who's making this movie?" Victoria asked, hands on hips again.

Sam, who had an answer for everything, gave a one-shouldered shrug.

That night, the shooting got promoted to national news. Civil rights activists, church leaders, and politicians all had opinions. Mom and Dad were at the hospital, so Nella was in charge of the TV. Her brothers called her a naked mole rat, but she kept it tuned to the news.

Just as she expected, the DeMarco house looked ugly and dreary. You couldn't tell how scrubbed and neat it was inside—inspection ready, Angela called it. You couldn't see Anthony's barbells or Angela's collection of little glass animals. All you could see was a house that looked exactly like where a murderer would live.

Mr. DeMarco stepped outside. He yelled at the camera. He slammed his door. A moment later, Victoria commanded the screen. She leaned into the microphone and said how extremely sorry she felt for Angela.

"She doesn't really have any friends."

"There's you, Nella!" Kevin pointed. "There's you, Vinny! Gross! Look at your snot rocket!"

Towering behind Victoria, Nella looked stupid as a statue. She and booger-faced Vinny gaped at the camera. Which made it appear she was agreeing with every word Victoria said. The evil microphone hovered in the air, so black it seemed to be absorbing all available light.

"Chief of Police Michael Corcoran is expected to announce tomorrow whether charges will be brought," Turquoise Suit said. "We'll be following this tragic case closely as it unfolds."

"You're on TV!" Bobby couldn't get over it. "Everybody in the whole world saw you."

Nella clicked the set off. Her brothers raged in protest, but she informed them that if they weren't in their beds by the count of five, unspeakable things would occur. They let her get all the way to four before they ran.

Collapsing on the couch, she felt sick. She'd spent all afternoon hoping against hope that when Angela peeked through the curtains, she hadn't noticed Nella in the crowd.

That hope was over now. Angela would watch the news. Angela would see her and Vinny, who Angela loved so much, and who loved her back so much—see them standing alongside Victoria. She'd see their stupid, blank stares as they agreed: Angela DeMarco didn't have any friends.

MARIE, AGAIN
then

Other graves were decorated for the holidays. Christmas wreathes, Easter lilies, miniature American flags, but Marie's was always bare. Whenever Nella visited, she left a pebble on the stone bench, a token that someone remembered.

One cloudy spring afternoon, as she rounded the bend in the path, she saw two pale legs sticking out from the bench. Motionless. Bloodless. Nella's heart froze in her chest.

Her lips formed the syllables. *Ma-rie.*

The feet levitated, then hit the ground.

"I thought you were a serial killer!" yelled Angela.

"I thought you were a ghost!" yelled Nella.

They both burst into semihysterics.

"What are you doing here?"

"What are *you* doing here?"

Nella picked up a pebble and set it beside the others on the back of the bench. Angela stopped laughing.

"You? You put all those there?"

"It's Marie," Nella whispered. "The girl my father . . ."

Angela looked from her to the statue and back again. "How do you know?" She whispered too.

"I can just tell. I . . . I recognize her."

They huddled together on the bench. Angela's jeans and sweatshirt needed to be washed, and her braids were fuzzy. She didn't smell that good, to tell the truth.

"That's why I'm here," Nella said. "What about you?"

"You know. My father. My house." Angela hunched her shoulders. She bit her thumb, which was what she did now to keep from sucking her hair. "I come here sometimes, just to get away. I'm not allowed, but way back here nobody ever sees me. Till you."

They both gazed at Marie.

"Nobody cares about her," Nella said softly. "They don't come see her or bring her flowers. It's so sad. It's like they abandoned her."

A soft breeze blew, and the shadows of new leaves flickered across the statue's cheeks and brow.

"It's like a fairy tale," whispered Angela. "She was reaching for something forbidden, and she got turned to stone. Now she's forced to reach forever."

"Not forever! That's too sad."

Angela jumped up and stood on tiptoe. For a second Nella thought she was imitating Marie. But Angela stretched higher yet and snapped off the tip of a tree branch. A dogwood, just coming into bud. Angela tried to put it in the statue's hand, but it slipped to the ground. Nella tugged the elastic out of her ponytail. Together they fastened the branch to the cool stone fingers.

They kept bringing Marie presents—a string of pearly rosary beads, a pinwheel from the Feast, a stick of Laffy Taffy. They did it because they felt sorry for her, forgotten and alone. They were too old to believe in magic. They knew that no matter how many offerings they brought, Marie would never come to life. Her cold white cheeks would never flush, her frozen lips would never move and say, *Thank you. You have remembered me when everyone else has forgotten. For your kindness, I will grant you each one wish.*

All that spring they came, and into the summer and fall. (Nella couldn't remember when they stopped.)

SEASHELL
now

Nonni couldn't talk.

Or she could, but no one understood her.

"Maybe Vinny can translate," Clem said over the phone. "Oh wait. Maybe that's not funny?"

It definitely was not, but how could Nella blame her? Clem might as well be in that galaxy far far away.

Holding the phone, Nella paced the backyard. Other things she somehow couldn't tell Clem included how what happened was her fault. And how scared she was that when she saw Nonni, her great-grandmother would miraculously regain her speech. She'd sit up in bed, point,

189

and shout in fury, "It's all her fault! Her, that lazy selfish *ragazza*!"

And D'Lon Andrews? Nella didn't even know where to begin.

They washed the blood off the sidewalk, but you could still tell. Would you always be able to tell?

Her brothers were digging behind the garage. They adored repetitive, meaningless activity. They could throw a ball against a wall for hours. They could practice karate kicks or dig a hole to nowhere all day long. Nella envied their Brainless Joy.

"I can't believe it about Anthony," said Clem, and Nella stopped pacing.

"You already know?"

"It's in the *New York Times*. Zoinks, Nell. Angela's brother! What was he like?"

"Not was! He still is! You sound like one of the stupid reporters."

The other end of the phone grew quiet. Nella heard a low whooshing sound, rhythmic and hypnotizing. The waves, she guessed. Nella had never seen an ocean. Clem had been to the Atlantic a million times, and also to the Pacific, and once to the Bering Sea.

"Anyway," said Clem.

"I'm sorry. You're not stupid." Nella watched Bobby

jump into the hole. It was amazingly deep—only his head showed over the edge.

"My mother says it's proof we need stricter gun-control laws."

"Don't be stupid! Anthony's allowed to have that gun." Nella had decided this, on her own. "It's part of his job."

"Patch says there's no justification for shooting an injured, unarmed man. He says racism is alive and well in this country."

"Anthony isn't racist! He used to have a black girlfriend. Your father doesn't know the first thing about Anthony!"

"You definitely don't need to shout, Nell."

"You definitely don't need to keep quoting your parents."

Silence again. Now Kevin jumped into the hole. Nella stepped to the edge and peered down. Her brothers were curled up like grubs. They didn't even notice her. She wasn't part of whatever make-believe world they were in. On the other end of the phone, the sea whooshed and sighed.

"I know you've known them a long time," Clem said. "That doesn't mean he's innocent."

"What?"

"I'm just saying. Maybe you need to look at the bigger picture."

"You mean like the *cosmic* picture?"

"That wasn't too sarcastic."

Nella listened to another oceanic sigh.

"Isn't there something you want to tell me?" asked Clem.

What could she possibly mean? "Didn't I already tell you enough?"

"Fine."

"I'm sorry," Nella said again. But she didn't really mean it. And she knew Clem could tell. FART.

"I'll call you tomorrow." Pause. "Approximately 1,768,000 seconds till I get back."

As soon as Nella clicked off, something strange happened. The whoosh of the ocean gave way to another low, hushed sound. This sound was sad and frightened, like a crying child rocking herself back and forth.

It's the wind, Nella told herself, even though not a single leaf stirred.

Later, Nella sat down at the computer and checked the news.

Anthony DeMarco Jr. was charged with voluntary manslaughter.

He would be arraigned tomorrow.

If convicted, he faced up to fifteen years.

Fifteen years. Longer than Nella's entire life.

She scrolled and clicked, scrolled and clicked. The story was getting reported everywhere. Yet nowhere could she find anyone, except for Mr. DeMarco, who said this must all be a big mistake.

Slaughter. She couldn't think of an uglier word.

The hushed sound once again filled Nella's ears, like she was holding up a seashell, one as big as the world.

What the Statue of Jeptha A. Stone Would Say if It Could

Truth #1: It is a mistake to lay eggs this time of year.
Truth #2: A bird's heart beats at a frightening rate.
Truth #3: Life can surprise you, even when you're dead.

LANDSLIDE
now

Police speculated that D'Lon Andrews fell asleep at the wheel and hit the cemetery wall at twenty-five to thirty miles per hour. He suffered head injuries as well as the gunshot wounds, the one to the abdomen judged to be fatal. Complete autopsy and toxicology reports were pending. Found in the dead man's pocket was a wallet containing a photo of his two sons. Ages four and two.

This photo got a lot of screen time.

The weapon Anthony DeMarco Jr. fired was not registered. It was not issued to him by Vigilant Security, the company where he is employed.

Was employed.

It appeared to have been illegally obtained. So far it could not be traced.

Anthony's court-appointed lawyer said her client didn't know about the car accident. Her client acted on what he saw: a menacing figure, a terrified neighbor. Her client had no further comments at this time.

There was a new photo: Anthony being arraigned. He wore one of those orange jumpsuits. Handcuffs. A stony-faced jailer on either side of him, as if they were guarding a dangerous criminal who might attempt escape any moment. Nella studied his face, trying to recognize anything in it. His deep-set eyes and full lips had slipped beneath a veil. A screen had gone up between him and the world, and Nella couldn't see in. She wondered if he could see out.

Zooming in, she could just make out the scar over his left eye.

Did handcuffs hurt?

"For the love of God. What was that kid doing with a gun?" Dad swore under his breath.

"He needs a good lawyer," Mom said. "But how will they ever afford that?"

Dad was home from visiting Nonni. The smell of the hospital clung to him—strong soap, gross food. After a visit there, he spoke the foreign language of doctors. He used mysterious abbreviations and quoted numbers and scores on tests. Dad tried to sound like an authority, but Nella could tell: he was just repeating what they told him. Nobody, maybe not even the doctors, could predict what Nonni's brain was going to do.

Mom looked so tired. When she frowned, she got a wrinkle that came to a point just above her nose, like the marking on some exotic bird.

"His bail's sky-high," Dad said. "They'll never be able to post it."

Vinny climbed into Mom's lap. It had been a long time since he'd nursed, but he patted her breast like they were old friends. Mom took his hand and pressed it between both of hers.

"Do you want some cereal? Do you want a banana?" Her voice was a little desperate, like she was talking to someone who spoke another language. Which she was.

When Vinny grinned, his eyes closed right up. His hair, which Mom still didn't have the heart to cut, was a tornado of curls. When he replied in gobbledegook, Dad echoed it back to him.

"We're supposed to talk in slow, clear English!" Mom scolded. "The doctor said."

"He's saying he loves you." Dad's face softened. He touched Mom's cheek. "It's clear as day to me."

"Ba-na-na," said Mom, holding one up. "Ap-ple." Bobby bounced into the room and grabbed the banana.

"Bobby," said Dad, "do you love Vinny?"

"Mostly."

"Why?"

"I don't know." Bobby looked suspicious.

"Try and say."

Bobby flattened his nose with his palm. "I just do, that's all."

"I rest my case." Dad pushed back his chair.

"What case?" said Mom.

"The things that matter most?" Dad paused in the doorway. His eyes met Nella's, then flicked away. "You don't need words. You just know."

Since Clem had left, Nella hadn't once gone on CRAPP patrol. Plastic bags lodged in the sidewalk trees, and bad thoughts in her mind. She couldn't pluck them out, not the bags or the thoughts.

Everyone was still on Anthony's side, but whispers started. Who really knew the first thing about him, after all? He had that girlfriend, remember. Maybe he got mixed up with people from her neighborhood. Maybe it was a gang thing. Gangs, drugs, crime—that's what went on down in that part of town. That's where you went when you wanted a gun with no questions asked.

Janelle lived up the hill in the Heights, Nella knew. She wasn't from *that part of town*.

And now they heard there was going to be a vigil at the Manzinis'. D'Lon Andrews's church and some other organizations were sponsoring it. By early evening, cars circled the streets, looking for parking spots. The neighborhood watched, uneasy. Why did they have to have the vigil here? What was wrong with their own neighborhood? What were they trying to prove?

Late that afternoon, on the way to Nonni's house, Nella stopped at Franny's. A jar on the counter was labeled ANTHONY DEMARCO JR. BALE FUND. It held a few bills and some change. Nella dug quarters and dimes out of her pocket and dropped them in. She trailed back out, behind two guys wearing muddy work boots and Hilltop Cemetery shirts. Probably summer hires, the college kids who drove Dad crazy.

"Who's Anthony DeMonte, anyway?" one of them asked, reaching in his bag for a doughnut.

"Some butthead from the neighborhood. He shot an unarmed black guy. Trying to be a hero!"

"Christ!" The guy shoved half the doughnut in his mouth. "What's wrong with these people?"

"Plenty. But they got doughnut making down."

Nella glared. The Fury of Nonni pulsed through her. She turned on her heel, immediately tripped, and hit the pavement. One of the guys offered her a hand.

"You okay?"

Nella got to her own feet. "He's not a butthead! And since you're so superior, why don't you do us all a favor and go away!"

The boy tucked his chin against his neck and stared. "Sor-ree!"

"She told you, loser," said the other one, grinning.

Nella dusted herself off and charged away, heart thudding. She couldn't believe she did that. She never told people off. But she was still furious.

And then it came to her: the stupid things those stupid guys said about Anthony—they were no different from the stupid things her stupid neighbors were saying about Janelle.

Nonni's house was like a crime scene. The broken coffee mug still lay on the kitchen floor. A crusty dish and glass of curdled milk still sat on the table. The garbage reeked. Nella swept, washed the dishes, and scrubbed out the can.

When she hauled the garbage to the curb, Hairy Boy and Turtle Girl were coming down their front steps. Turtle Girl stopped and called to Nella.

"Hey. The lady who lives there? Is she your grandma?"

"No," said Nella, technically not a lie. She hurried back inside.

She gathered the things on the list Dad gave her: underwear, lipstick, photographs, rosary beads. Every drawer she opened had a bag of candy stashed in the back, and Nella took some Laffy Taffy, in case the rehab center where they were transferring her didn't serve sweets.

Next Nella went to Clem's. She watered the tomatoes, though they didn't need it, and worked Mr. T's program. By now he let her scoop him up, and never spurted green poop on her. Tonight he made a sniffing sound that sounded like *You're okay*. When she fed him, he grunted like a minuscule pig. *This is delicious.* Even hedgehogs, it seemed, yearned to communicate.

Nella sat on Clem's bed. The glow-in-the-dark stars looked innocent and hopeful, like a remnant of some happy, ancient civilization. If only you could store up happiness. Dig a hole or keep it in a happiness piggy bank.

Clem's digital clock blinked forward. She jumped up.

Outside, Nella didn't recognize the sound. The wind, maybe? Except the trees behind the stone wall didn't move. A flock of birds with heavy wings? Except the sky was empty. Ghosts? Except of course that was ridiculous. A girl who'd lived her whole life across from a graveyard did not let herself believe in ghosts.

The July night was warm, but she shivered. Until a few days ago, Nella knew every sight and sound, smell and taste of her neighborhood. The steep hill and narrow houses, the cheesy music at Mama Gemma's, the supernatural perfume of fresh doughnuts, and the zing of lemon ice. She and Angela used to love— No. Don't think about Angela. Just don't.

The world tilted and went blurry.

"You okay?" asked a soft voice at her elbow.

A stranger. A woman with long dreads and dark, anxious eyes. Nella had almost reached the street where it happened, and suddenly she was surrounded by other people, all intent on getting to the source of that sound. Looking into the woman's concerned face, Nella at last recognized what that sound was. Voices. Voices singing.

"I'm all right," said Nella, and then, who knew why, she said thank you in Italian. *"Mille grazie."*

The woman hesitated, but the sound, the singing, was pulling her too. She reached up—Nella was taller than she was—and gave Nella's head a motherly pat. Then disappeared around the corner.

Police cars blocked off the street. Cops leaned against them, arms folded. Maybe they were here to protect people, but they scared Nella. There were news vans, men with cameras on their shoulders. She looked around, recognizing no one. A tornado snatched up every person she knew and spun them away. An earthquake gobbled them down. A landslide pulverized them.

She slipped between the barricades. A sea of strangers overflowed the narrow street, spilling onto the sidewalks and little front lawns. Nella kept searching for a familiar face, but the only one she found was Father Gomez, who stood near the Manzinis' front door. The family was gone—they left the day after it happened, to stay with relatives in the suburbs. Next to Father Gomez was a man in a big-brimmed black hat, and other men and women with somber faces. A short black man in a robe led a choir that swayed as it sang. All around her, people joined in, but Nella didn't recognize the hymn. It was mournful and beautiful, making her think of a river. For a moment she fell under its spell, but then she was afraid. These strangers had to hate Anthony. Invaders, she thought, just as someone put a hand on her arm. Nella spun around, heart racing. A woman with a round, sad face was holding out an unlit candle.

"Here, sugar," she said.

"Oh," said Nella. "Thank you." Then heard herself repeat, *"Mille grazie."*

Father Gomez took the microphone. His accent was heavy and the microphone squealed, so it was hard to understand most of what he said, but people nodded politely, and when he called on Our Heavenly Father to heal us in our suffering and pain, the round-faced woman beside her whispered, "Amen."

Nella stood on her toes, hoping Sister Rosa was here too. But no. She was banished to the rest home. The other white people looked like they were from up the hill. Some held signs. STOP THE VIOLENCE and HATE BREEDS HATE and pictures of guns with red lines through them. Near a bed of flowers with a statue of St. Francis in the middle, Hairy Boy had his arm around Turtle Girl. She was crying, and so were other girls Nella could tell were students.

The landslide. People from up the hill had come sliding down. Against the laws of physics, people from down the hill had come surging up. Nella's neighborhood had gotten scraped away.

Father Gomez gave the microphone to a woman who introduced herself as their city councilwoman. Her voice was as clear as Father Gomez's was muddled.

"My friends, we gather here tonight to mourn a young man who had all his life ahead of him. D'Lon dreamed of graduating from college. He dreamed of marrying the woman he loved, and making a home for the two little boys who meant more to him than life itself. He dreamed of a future shining with possibilities.

"But those dreams have been cruelly snatched away. Now we will never know who D'Lon Andrews could have become, or what he could have accomplished."

A man near Nella lowered his head into his hands. Someone behind her whispered a prayer.

"Yet another young, promising black man has gone to a violent, premature death. My friends, tonight we gather here in deepest sorrow and pain."

A young woman and two little boys stood off to the side. D'Lon's fiancée—Nella recognized her from TV. And those were the boys in the photograph shown so often. The older one, wearing a too-big football jersey, gripped his mother's skirt. The younger, Vinny-sized one crouched to pick up something bright lying in the grass. A toy—it must have belonged to the Manzinis' daughter. He looked at it with surprise and delight, like it fell from the sky just for him.

"We gather here tonight in sorrow, but not entirely in shock. We have seen tragedies like this far too many times before. Each time we hope and pray it will be the last time, and yet here we are again. How can we let this keep happening? How can we refuse to learn?" The councilwoman held out her arms. "This is a question we cannot afford to continue asking. This is a question that we need to answer."

All around Nella, people murmured. The bag of Nonni's underwear and candy tried to slip from her arms but she caught it.

"My friends, D'Lon is gone, but tonight, I can hear his voice. While we falter and fumble for words, I hear him calling out to us. I hear him begging us to work together to eradicate prejudice and misunderstanding, and to replace them with equality and compassion."

"Amen," voices answered. "Amen!"

"I hear him asking us to mend these terrible divisions between us, and put a stop, once and for all, to violence. I hear him calling out, *Bury the hatred! Promise your children this will never happen again.*"

"Anthony doesn't hate anyone," Nella whispered.

Another hand touched her and made her jump, startled and afraid. But it was just a girl about her age, who held her lit candle to Nella's unlit one. "Pass it on," she said as the flame bent and leaped.

Nella turned and touched her candle to the next person's. The flame passed from hand to hand, flickering in the dark, and now the choir was singing again, and everyone was joining in, voices rising and blending. Nella heard the voice of the girl beside her, and behind her another voice that twisted and twined upward till it burst on the air like some great, fragrant flower. All around her, people sang.

This hymn Nella recognized. She could sing too, but her throat had gone dry. Instead, she turned around. Candle in one hand, Nonni's underwear and candy in the other, Nella stumbled through the crowd. The singing was a powerful river rising all around her, trying to sweep her up. Looking back, she saw the Vinny-sized son playing with the toy he found. His Bobby-sized brother put a finger to his lips and frowned. Nella's heart thunked against her ribs. Tears dimmed her eyes. Her feet pretzeled and she bumped into a man who caught her elbow.

"Sorry," she said. "So sorry!"

She finally made her way out of the crowd, and there stood Angela. The streetlight fell across her face. Her skin was the color of a plant trying to grow where no sun reached. But most disturbing of all was her hair. It fell in a single uneven braid down her back. Her part was crooked. She stared at Nella's candle.

"I . . ." Nella wanted to explain, but how could she? She didn't understand herself. "I . . . I didn't mean to go. I just, somehow I did." She blew out the candle. "It's not like I think . . . I know he didn't mean it, Angela. I know he'd never."

Angela looked tired, too tired to argue. Or maybe she

didn't care anymore what Nella thought.

"Are you . . . are you okay?" Nella asked. Even for someone whose specialty was the wrong question, this was awful.

The singing faded away. Silence took over. People bowed their heads. The candles shone in the dark. The silence had a solid, impenetrable shape. Nella and Angela stood on the outside of it, looking in.

Or Nella did. When she turned around, Angela had disappeared.

At home, Mom and Dad were watching the news. They didn't notice Nella hovering in the doorway, where she viewed the vigil all over again, this time through the eyes of the camera. It zeroed in on the fiancée's stricken face, the son gripping his mother's skirt. It showed the councilwoman raising her hands to the sky and saying she heard D'Lon's voice still speaking. It showed an old man with tears rolling down his lined face.

It showed what it chose to and left out everything else.

"This neighborhood's decades-old history of segregation and racial strife has come back to haunt it," said the reporter, who tonight wore a black suit. Behind her, the crowd started to sing. "Meanwhile, civil rights groups are calling for stiffer charges against Anthony DeMarco Jr., who remains in jail."

Dad clicked the remote. He sat rigid, staring at the blank screen, till Mom slipped her arm around him.

"It's okay," she said. "I'm here. I'm always here."

Dad leaned into her and let his head rest on her shoulder. Mom rubbed his back and said soft, soothing things, the way she did to Nella and her brothers when they were scared or hurt. Seeing her father like that made Nella's heart twist, and she was back in that crowd, surrounded by people she didn't know, their beautiful, aching voices rising up to heaven, trying to push away what couldn't be moved.

What the Statue of
Jeptha A. Stone
Would Say if It Could

My merry bird is unnaturally quiet.

It's as if she perceives some disturbance in the celestial sphere.

NONNI, TIME TRAVELER
now

Where was the pleasant lake of Pleasant Lake Nursing and Rehab Center? It couldn't possibly be that muddy pond ringed with goose poop.

In the elevator, Dad took Nella's hand, something he hadn't tried to do in years.

Nella let him.

The hallway was crowded with food carts, an industrial floor washer, empty wheelchairs. When Nella glanced into the rooms, she saw bony bare feet at the ends of beds. In one doorway, a man or a woman, she couldn't tell which, sat in a wheelchair and stared. Nella's dread deepened.

Dad still held her hand, and she was glad.

"Grarrr," said Nonni. "Waa gwaa."

Like a hawk flapping a broken wing. A powerful witch who'd forgotten her spells. One side of Nonni's face still drooped, though not as badly. She made more noises. A chair scraping the floor, or distant geese honking—that was what it sounded like, not words.

How could Nella tell she wanted water? How could she understand? She just could, the same way Bobby understood Vinny. She reached for the plastic pitcher on the bedside table, but Nonni shook out more garbled sounds. Nella knew: the water was too warm. An aide pointed her toward the lounge where there was a refrigerator. The ball game played on a TV, and a man in a ball cap snored on the couch in front of it. Nella stalled as long as she could, not wanting to go back. Nonni helpless was way worse than Nonni furious.

Dad looked relieved to see her. Nella put the straw to her great-grandmother's dry lips. Without her lipstick, she was so colorless she all but disappeared into the pillow. No way she was going to accuse Nella of anything. She was much too weak. Maybe she couldn't even remember what happened.

Her hand on the covers was a map, her veins twisting blue rivers. Nella watched her eyelids flutter, and hoped she was dreaming of somewhere else. Perching in the persimmon tree with her brother, Carlo, or grinding up spices for homemade sausage. Nella hoped Nonni was time traveling, far away from this place.

"I couldn't understand a word out of her," Dad said in the car. His voice was choked with sadness.

Nella remembered what he said about Vinny. *Words don't matter.* But he was wrong. Without words, you were only partly connected. Too much had to stay locked inside.

A voice. Nella had never known how much having a voice mattered.

THIS VOICE INSIDE
then

E nglish is a ridiculous language," Nella said. It was an
afternoon a few months after she and Clem had met.
"Like infinite and infinitesimal. One means huge and the
other means microscopic. How can that be?"

Clem, doodling in a sketchbook, shrugged.

"What are words, anyway?" Nella went on. "If you listen to a language you don't know, it's pure gibberish. Just
vowels and consonants arranged in senseless, random ways.
The only reason it makes sense is because people decide it
does. Otherwise it's just noise!"

Clem sat up, interested now. "Like time," she said.

"Like how we keep trying to measure it and calculate it, when it's the most slippery, mysterious thing that exists."

"You know what else makes no sense?" Nella was on a roll. "God having no beginning and no end. I get the no ending—that's what heaven is. But it's impossible to have no beginning."

"That one's easy." Clem's pencil traced a circle in the air. "Think of a toy train track that goes round and round so you can't tell where it starts and where it ends."

"God is not a toy train track!"

"Chill!" Clem grinned. "I'm not insulting God!"

Where did Nella's questions come from? Did everyone have this voice inside, asking questions? But people were so different. It couldn't be the same voice. Everyone's must be programmed differently, like the GPS voice. But where did it *come from*? Whose voice was it, really, popping up when you didn't expect, causing trouble and confusion? Coming from you but not being you?

More questions. Questions about questions. It was hopeless.

WITH A CAPITAL F
now

The autopsy report said that D'Lon Andrews died of a bullet wound to the abdomen. It also showed head injuries, probably from the car crash. The report said those injuries could account for his confusion and erratic behavior.

Clustering in the steamy midsummer air outside church, batting away mosquitoes at the bocce court, leaning across the tables at the social club, people talked. Business was down the tubes. The restaurants were half empty. Nobody wanted a Little Italy T-shirt, a Perry Como CD, a baby bib that said *Mangia!*, or a doormat

216

that said *Ciao!* It was as if the neighborhood had a bad smell. The Manzinis' front lawn was covered with candles and stuffed animals and bunches of wilted flowers. Protesters stood outside the DeMarco house all day, holding signs, praying and singing and sometimes shouting. One morning the telephone poles were plastered with signs: BOYCOTT RACISM. The smoke shop guys tore them down and ripped them to bits.

Mr. DeMarco tried to borrow the bail money, but his credit was no good. He already had a second mortgage on the house and was up to his eyeballs in debt. While he was in the service, his wife had emptied out their savings.

How people knew this, when Mr. DeMarco wouldn't talk to anyone, when it was even hard to tell if he and Angela were still hunkered inside that house, was not exactly clear.

Mrs. DeMarco? The runaway mother? Who knew? Maybe she was in a mental institution. Or was a drug addict. Or worse.

"Trouble breeds trouble," said a woman on the church steps. She shook her head like *What a shame, what a terrible shame*, but her upper lip curled as if she'd just bit something rotten.

A faker with a capital *F*.

Nella hurried inside and knelt down. God offers us choices, Sister Rosa would say. He hopes we will do right, but He leaves it up to us. We are born with the gift of free will.

But really? Most of life didn't feel like that. Where and when you were born. Who you got for parents. Whether you were pretty or not, smart or not, black or white or brown. Whether you happened to be at the wrong place at the wrong time and made one mistake and afterward nothing was ever the same. You couldn't choose or control any of these enormous, important things. What if God only tricked people into thinking they had choices? He was God. He could do whatever He wanted.

Though that would make God a faker too. And Nella wasn't buying that.

Beside the altar, the red sanctuary lamp glowed. It was always lit, never allowed to go out. It meant God dwelled here. This was His sacred space. Nella bowed her head. She closed her eyes.

One second! That was all it took for Anthony to pull that trigger. All the rest of his life, he was good and kind.

What's one second to you, eternal God? Just a tiny spark from a fire that never, ever goes out. You are infinite, and we are infinitesimal.

The Mass began. The old lady sitting behind Nella bellowed the responses at the top of her lungs, as if God was as hard of hearing as she was.

* * *

More than a thousand people attended the funeral. They held it in a big church downtown, and still people had to stand outside and listen to it broadcast over loudspeakers. The day was hot. People fainted.

Nella watched on TV. The sons wore suits and ties, and the little one kept looking down at himself, like he wasn't sure who this person was.

"We thank God for the short but blessed time we had with D'Lon," said the minister. "We thank God for all the love he gave, and the happy memories he left behind. Because of him, we are here together today, grieving yet fortified by faith. Faith and hope."

Dad always said that funerals were for the living, not the dead. Coming together, sharing memories, crying and laughing, people remembered that they were still alive.

"Let our hearts be free of hate today. Let us search our hearts and find forgiveness." The minister raised his arms to heaven. "Lord, we pray to you—help us find our way."

"Amen," Nella whispered.

WHY GOD
MADE SO MANY OF US
now

Newspapers lay uncollected on the DeMarco driveway, and the strip of front lawn grew ragged. Mr. Ferraro claimed he offered to mow it, but Tony DeMarco threatened to drill him in the butt if he didn't get off the property in the next three seconds. That was the thanks you got for trying to do your Christian duty.

The gossip enraged Dad. Why couldn't everyone shut their traps and mind their own business? He hauled his power mower over and cut the strip of grass within an inch of its life, and nobody threatened to drill his butt.

The ignoramuses dug more holes. They lay in ambush

under the front porch, machine-gunning anyone who passed by. They beat each other with blow-up baseball bats, and challenged each other to head-butting contests. They led a Meaningless Existence, and were happy.

Not Sal, though. Lately, he went off with other boys his age, which broke Kevin's heart.

The line between Mom's eyes cut deeper every day. Pretty soon, what was left of her beauty would be entirely used up.

That afternoon Dad had back-to-back burials, so Nella went alone to see Nonni. Mom disapproved, but Nella, to her own surprise, was determined to go. She took the city bus up the hill, the gates of Dr. Patchett's university on one side, the cemetery on the other. The bus chugged past the art school, where summer students had their easels set up outside, and a model in a long red dress lay in the grass with her head propped on her hand. The only time Nella had ever been to the art museum was on a school field trip, where a guide talked at them like they had mush for brains. The bus sputtered past a boy and girl standing under a tree, kissing like it was their job.

Then came the big houses with the wide lawns, the quiet, tree-lined streets where no one was out. It was like scenery for a movie, though Nella knew real people lived here. Maybe any foreign place felt fake? Because the people who lived there couldn't be like you. They must have different ideas, care about different things. But mostly because you knew: you did not belong here.

The bus sped up and Nella thought of the bottom of the hill, D'Lon Andrews's neighborhood, where the houses were as small and close together as hers. On the surface, the two neighborhoods had so much in common.

But it didn't feel that way. It felt as if there was a wall between his neighborhood and hers. The wall was invisible, and somehow that made it worse. It was harder to find your way past something you couldn't see.

Nella wasn't prejudiced. She wasn't ancient and ignorant like Nonni.

But now she remembered the night of the vigil, and the woman who tried to comfort her, and the girl who handed her a candle, and how even when she recognized the hymn they sang, she didn't join in. Nella pressed her forehead to the window glass and her throat got a strange ache, like it was wishing it had. Like there was a song in there that wanted to be heard.

Nella tried telling funny stories about her brothers, but Nonni just stared at the wall. When the physical therapist came in, Nonni refused to do her exercises. It wasn't like she was being stubborn. More like she had no energy, for anything, even fighting.

Nella remembered watching Nonni make lasagna. She had a crazy technique where she laid the cooked noodle flat on her arm, spread the filling, then rolled it up, wrist to elbow. It was how her mother taught her, back in the Abruzzi.

Dad had given Nella a Strict Warning: Whatever you do, don't mention Anthony. Nonni had no memory of the morning of the stroke, and bringing it up would make her upset. It would set back her progress.

What progress?

Usually the obituaries were Nonni's favorite newspaper feature, but when Nella started to read them aloud, Nonni shook her head. TV? No. Nella described how the barbarians set up a stand to sell rocks, and Hairy Boy actually took pity on them and bought some. She waited for Nonni to flicker to mean-spirited life—Hairy Boy? What means Hairy Boy? But no. Nothing. *Nulla.* She simply lay there, waiting for Nella to give up and go away.

Once, this was something that Nella would have been more than happy to do. But now she waited, now it was a waiting contest, till at last Nonni's eyes closed and she drifted off to sleep.

Nella smoothed the blanket.

"Everything's too mixed up," she whispered. "It's like . . . like nobody's in control of anything. Sister Rosa would say God is. But what if He's not?"

Nonni made no reply. She used to snort and snuffle in her sleep, because she couldn't stand to be ignored even when unconscious. But now Nella had to watch the rise and fall of the blanket to make sure she was still alive.

Nella suddenly felt so old. Maybe growing up wasn't smooth and steady? Maybe it happened in lurches and leaps and she had just aged. At last she stood up, tripped over an invisible gnome, and stepped out into the hallway.

Where she could not believe her eyes.

"Sister?" It was as if Nella had conjured up the sight. As if Sister Rosa was a mirage in the desert.

"Darling child!" That honeyed voice! It was truly her, and she was just as surprised as Nella. "What are you doing here?"

First Nella explained, then Sister.

"Visiting nursing homes is my new ministry." She wore her familiar gray skirt and vest and the big silver cross, but in place of her black lace-up shoes she had bright pink Crocs. She held one out for Nella to admire.

"For my bunions," she said, then smiled and added, "For fun, too."

Sister having fun—who could predict? Sister, that's

who. She trusted that God had a plan for her, and so He did. As they walked down the hallway, she stopped to compliment a woman's track suit and to pick up the paper dropped by a man pushing a walker. Sister's bright pink step was light. Her laugh was at the ready. Nella got jealous. She thought Sister's life would be over without her school and students, but it turned out she liked old people as much as young ones. She was an omni-people-liker.

"If you can wait a bit, I'll give you a ride home," Sister said.

"You can drive?"

"In a manner of speaking."

So Nella waited in the lobby, among the silk flowers and old-timey paintings, till Sister had visited all her people and was ready to go. The car, which belonged to the order, was enormous. It had fuzzy red seats and a statue of St. Christopher, Patron Saint of Travelers, stuck to the dashboard. Perched on a pillow, Sister played soft rock, and it was so peaceful inside that car, Nella almost fell asleep. Actually, she did fall asleep, and only woke up when she felt the car slow. Opening her eyes, she realized they were on the hill.

"Oh dear," said Sister. "Oh mercy."

She hit the brakes. The usual group of protesters stood outside the DeMarco house. They looked hot and tired, gripping their signs in the sun. One man, with long stringy hair, stood apart. Shouting.

"Oh mercy," repeated Sister. "This is not good."

"They're always there," said Nella. "Anthony . . ."

"I know, dear. I've been praying for them around the clock."

The shouting man began to whip his head from side to side, his long hair lashing his face. The words *hellfire* and *Jesus* were getting a good workout.

"This won't do," said Sister.

Before Nella could blink, Sister jumped out of the car. Her Crocs sped toward the man, who was windmilling his arms like he meant to land a knockout punch. He was big and heavy and definitely crazy—one whack and Sister would be flat on the ground.

The other protesters lowered their signs. A man wearing a white shirt moved forward, but Sister barreled past him, stopping a few inches from the shouting man. He squinted like he was trying to decide if she was real or a delusion. Nella held her breath. Without warning, the man swung his head sideways and lunged, grabbing the cross around Sister's neck. Nella jumped out of the car just as he yanked the cross toward his mouth. Sister tottered helplessly. He'd bite! He'd spit! Nella ran toward them, and the white-shirted protester moved in.

But Sister began speaking, so softly Nella couldn't make out what she said, and the man seemed to listen. He still gripped her cross, but his face unclenched, and his eyes seemed to focus. Sister's voice was low and gentle and continuous, and now, in slow motion, the man lifted her cross to his lips. Tenderly, as if it was his long-lost child. When Sister touched his arm, his head fell forward, and Nella watched the anger drain out of him, making an anger pool at his feet.

Now they were walking to the car, Sister was opening the back door, and the man was getting in. As she climbed behind the wheel, Sister arched her eyebrows at Nella.

"Whew!" she whispered.

A minute later they were pulling up in front of Nella's house. In the backseat, the man mumbled to himself. He stank of sweat and something else. What was Sister going to do with him?

"Will you be okay?" Nella asked.

"Me? It's our friend we have to worry about. But I know just where to get him a hot meal and some clean clothes."

"You're so brave. You didn't even think, just jumped right out and . . . You were like a superhero."

"Me?" Sister smiled. "What about you? Riding the bus all alone to look after your poor Nonni!"

"Sister, what did you say to him?"

"Say?" Sister's brow wrinkled. She shifted on her pillow. "I don't even remember. He just needed to hear a kind voice, that was all."

Nella got out of the car, and Sister leaned out the window.

"Remember, Nella. We need one another almost as much as we need God. Why else do you think He made so many of us?"

CAMERA'S EYE
now

"C"an you believe the stuff all those people are posting about Anthony?" Clem asked over the phone.

"What people? What stuff?"

"Never mind. They're all cretin trolls."

"Cretin trolls?"

Salvatore and Kevin were parked on the family computer. Getting them off would require explosives or highly expensive bribery, so Nella told Mom she had to go to the library. Bobby begged to come, which meant Vinny had to come, so here she was trying to steer the dilapidated stroller up the hill. She didn't dare suggest they buy a new one. She needed to believe this was the family's absolute last baby.

It was a thousand degrees out, and Bobby commenced whining immediately, so Nella had to tow him like a boat. Past the university gates, along the rows of cute, expensive shops, and finally to the library, where the air conditioning bathed them in bliss. She settled the boys in the play area and was lucky enough to snag a one-hour computer.

Going to the local news site, she found the latest article on Anthony and scrolled down to the comments.

Shoot first, then ask questions. Takes brains, Mario!

Everybody knows Little Italy is crawling with maggots and bigots. What do you expect?

Vinny toddled over, holding out a toy dish with plastic food. Nella pretended to gnaw a chicken leg.

Tell me that guy wasn't on drugs. They're all on drugs.

Someone else had posted a link to an article from— wait. Nella needed paper and pencil to figure out how long ago. Over forty years ago. It was about race riots in the Garfield neighborhood. Stores were looted, cars were burned. The National Guard was called in, and the photos looked like a war in some other country. People were shot, and some died.

Nella leaned forward. She read how Little Italy formed its own armed guard, teams of men patrolling around the clock. Late one night, two of them spotted a man sitting in a parked car at the bottom of the hill. Back then, there was a big lumberyard down there, and they became convinced that the man, who was black, meant to set it on fire. Somehow shots got fired. Somehow the black man was dead.

The faces of the smoke shop men flashed through her mind.

Vinny was back with a plastic green bean in each fist. He solemnly set them on her knees.

Now she read how the shooters claimed they were just protecting their families. They were quickly acquitted, and the city councilman commented, "If only that guy had stayed home where he belonged, none of this would have happened."

Nella started to feel light-headed. The stories were about another neighborhood, not hers.

Great-uncle Vito on his big horse. A horse with hooves the size of a newborn's head.

She read how outraged Little Italy was when black students were bused into the neighborhood school, how the school eventually got closed down. (This was the school where Clem lived now, where the smell of chalk still swirled through the halls.) She read about rocks thrown at passing cars, a beating behind Mama Gemma's. Another Feast disrupted by fistfights.

Vinny brought her a fried egg, and she was so dazed she actually bit it. She knew there'd been troubles, but Mom said they were exaggerated. Did she remember wrong? But wait— she wasn't even born then. All her parents knew was what they'd heard, the stories passed down to them, other people's memories. *Mi ricordo. I remember.* She thought how Dad couldn't remember any other mother except Nonni. That was wrong, but for him it was true. He'd rewritten the past.

The past was the past. Except maybe not.

Maybe people were like cameras. They saw what they focused on, and left out all the rest.

Nell's brain spun. It tried to piece these bits together, to make some sense of it, but all she got was more questions. What if D'Lon had been white, not black? Would Anthony still have shot him? Would he have tried harder to figure out what was happening? Would he have been so scared, so angry, so whatever he was?

Her computer session was almost over, but she read a few more comments.

> What a stinking, salami-sucking, grease-ball. Jes' sayin'.

232

DeMarco will get off, don't kid yourself. The Mafia
still calls the shots.

They called Anthony "Gino" and "wop." They said he
deserved his own bullet. Clutching her fried egg, Nella's
confusion went deeper.

This is about me, too, she realized. *Me and my family.
They're calling us and everyone in the neighborhood those
names too.*

We don't deserve that.

Do we?

The computer went blank. It was reserved for someone
else, and she stumbled to her feet. Now Vinny brought her
a book about a little girl and her toy digger, and she read
it to him and Bobby three times in a row. The librarians
beamed at her. Such a good sister! Afterward, she pushed
the wretched stroller back down the hill and used her last
bit of money to buy them rocket pops, which turned them
into ecstatic, blue-lipped aliens.

A bird dipped low, flashing yellow wings. Goodness
felt as small, as flitting as that bird. Hatred and evil were
much louder and more powerful. They lasted and lasted,
and even time couldn't rub them out. Nella tried to think
what Sister Rosa would say, but today that honeyed voice
was too faint and frail.

GAD
now

Angela's phone rang and rang.

Look at the caller ID. It's me!

"Nella?"

"Oh, Angela! I was scared you wouldn't answer."

"What do you want?"

"What?" She expected Angela to be happy to hear from her. Even grateful. "I just wanted to check how . . . Did you go visit Anthony?"

"*That's* why you called." Angela's voice was brittle. "I know you're in love with him. It's the only reason you were friends with me."

"What?" Nella jumped up from her porch chair. "That's not true!"

"You haven't called me in forever. So why now?" Angela's voice turned so steely, Nella barely recognized it.

Angela had once explained about the body armor combat soldiers wear. Metallic, bullet-resistant vests with extra protection over the heart. Helmets made of something called Kevlar, and all of it so heavy you wouldn't think a person could walk, let alone run. Angela said sometimes it seemed like her father still wore his. He traded the real stuff for invisible armor, so nobody could get to him.

Even the people who loved him.

"You just want in on the excitement," Angela said. "Now that my brother's a famous murderer."

"No!" Nella was horrified. "I don't think he's a murderer!"

"Then you're the only one! Strangers call us up. They mail him death threats. We can't even step one foot outside."

"That's terrible!"

"Other people thank him for shooting. They say . . . You wouldn't believe what they say."

"Yes I would. I went online and I saw."

"The worst thing is my father . . ."

"What? Your father what?"

Silence. Nella's heart was loud in her ears.

"Never mind. He's fine. Everything's okay. I have to go now. Thanks for calling."

"Angela? Please tell me."

But she had hung up.

Mom came out on the porch, stretched her arms, and cocked her head at Nella.

"Who were you talking to?" she asked.

"I don't know," said Nella.

Right now, she wasn't even exactly sure who she was.

The "bale" jar wasn't even half full. Someone had dropped their old chewing gum in. As Nella turned to leave, she almost crashed into Sam Ferraro.

"Reckless driving." He grabbed her arm. "You're under arrest."

"You are so not funny."

To her surprise, he followed her back outside. "You don't look good," he said. Which she was sure was true. Which made her not care what happened next.

"I was all wrong," she blurted.

"Okay."

"I thought the world was mostly good. Like if you did one of those graphs that look like a pie, the bad part would be just a sliver compared to the good part. But it's the other way around."

Most people would run for their lives. Or at least sloooowly back away. Sam stood his ground, and Nella remembered that time in religion class he told Sister Rosa that you didn't need to believe in God to be good. Everyone thought he was just showing off, trying to get Sister upset, but to their amazement, Sister agreed with him. All you needed, she said, was to know how to see through eyes other than your own. That, and some courage.

"Like, could you give a specific example?" he asked now.

"Like, I called Angela." As soon as she said it, Nella realized what upset her the most about the phone conversation. "She sounded cold and hard. She sounded like her father."

"Her father's a waste of space." His glance flicked away. "Mine is too, a lot of the time."

"But I remember when he wasn't. When we were, like, five, Mr. DeMarco taught me how to toast a perfect golden marshmallow. My father had already taught me, but I pretended I didn't know, because I didn't want to hurt his feelings. He used to take us to the playground and push us on the swings."

"You're the only one who was ever friends with her. It's not like anybody else really cared."

"I did care!"

"That's what I just said." His eyes crinkled when he smiled, and Nella suddenly realized she wasn't bending her knees, yet she was looking right into those eyes. Which were the color of chocolate kisses. Sam had grown. Since summer started, he'd gotten as tall as she was. She turned away so he wouldn't see her blush.

"I have to go see a hedgehog."

"I'm in!"

Nella hesitated, but what harm could it do?

Sam couldn't believe the Patchetts' house. He tried out the couch, the low-slung chair covered in sheepskin, the big balancing ball Mrs. Patchett used for a desk chair. When Nella called him Goldilocks, he laughed. Nella's cheeks did their Duraflame imitation. Making Sam laugh—she could get addicted to that.

"What the freak?" Looking around at Clem's stuff, he got a funny expression. "It looks like a guy's room."

"That is so ignorant. What century are you from?" Nella showed him Mr. T, curled up into a spiny ball in a corner of his tank.

"A cactus for a pet," he said. "A cactus critter. Yikes! You're not really going to touch him?"

"You have to be Gentle and Decisive." She lifted the lid off the cage.

"Is that a quote from Sister Rosa or something?"

"It could be." It was Nella's turn to laugh. Mr. Tiggy-winkle bristled, but she said his name softly, held her fingers near his pointy nose. Sam moved so close she smelled his clean-T-shirt smell. Sliding her fingers under Mr. T's soft belly, she scooped him into her palm. One prickle, two—but it was worth it to see Sam jump back, eyes wide.

"He can't eject those things, can he?"

Little by little, the hedgie uncurled. He poked out his head. His nose twitched. His face was beyond sweet.

"Aw," said Sam, such a tender sound Nella all but dropped Mr. T. It was like Sam just told her a secret.

Sam had to be the one to feed him. He refilled the water, too. They stood side by side, listening to Mr. T make happy, piggy grunts. Sam told her how cute his dog was when he was a puppy.

"Now he's so old, he just lies around making toxic farts." Sam paused. "I still love him, though."

Nella couldn't believe he'd said *love*. Even about a dog. Boys didn't use that word, at least not in public. Which made her understand, *This was private.*

When she turned to look at him, he had two noses.

"Umm . . ."

(Later, Nella would think that Clem's bedroom was the perfect place for what happened next. Which was a kind of cosmic event. Also, later, she would be astonished that

Sam's lips could be that soft, as soft as her baby brother's.)

Right now all she could think was . . . nothing. The space formerly inhabited by her brain filled with gold-spun air as Sam Ferraro gave her a kiss.

CHOOSE YOUR OWN ADVENTURE
then and now

Mom clasped Nella's small hand firmly in hers and started clipping. Bits of fingernail flew. Nella hated this. Why didn't God make fingernails permanent? What was the use of growing them when they just had to get clipped?

"You next," said Mom, reaching for Angela's hand. But as usual her nails were bitten down to nothing.

That day, Mom read to them. They leaned in close on either side, and Nella could feel the baby—which baby?—kicking inside her mother's big, hard belly.

It was a Choose Your Own Adventure book, which

Nella disliked, but it was so rare Mom had time to read to her, she pretended to love it. Angela was the one who protested.

"Couldn't the author make up his own mind?"

Mom laughed. "I'm sure he could. But he wanted to let you decide."

"No." Angela made her stubborn face. "It's his job."

"That's right," said Nella. "He's supposed to know how things turn out. Not us."

The baby—it was Bobby—kicked like he agreed, and they all burst out laughing.

Years later, lying beneath the artificial, glow-in-the-dark galaxy, Clem asked if Nella believed in fate.

"Sort of," said Nella. "I mean, yes. Do you?"

"I think it's more like those Choose Your Own Adventure books, where the reader gets to pick the plot."

"I hate those books! An author should write one ending and stick with it. That's his duty."

"So you mean writers are like God? I'm not insulting God! Just asking."

"Well, yes." Nella had actually always imagined God with a big book, everyone's story written down.

"I read an interview with this writer who said she never knows what's going to happen. She said her characters were always hijacking the plot and surprising her."

"Maybe that's true for human writers," Nella said. "But God already knows everything. You can't surprise Him."

"Being God must be so boring."

Nella refused to speak to her the rest of the day.

STICKS AND STONES
now

Holding a book, Vinny climbed into her lap. All he wanted to do was turn pages, but Nella wouldn't let him. She pointed at a picture.

"What's that? What do you see? Say *carrot*. What's that? Say *bunny*."

Did Vinny know he couldn't talk? Or did he think he was actually making sense? His baby brow furrowed as he stared at the page. What if something really was wrong with his brain? What if he didn't grow out of this but was always behind, the kid who was not quite right? She tightened her arm around him.

"Fish," she insisted. "Say *fish*!"

Salvatore sat beside them. "Eel," he told Vinny. "Say electric eel." Suddenly, he sat back. He looked stricken. "Anthony's going to fry in the electric chair."

"What? Who said that?"

"People."

"Don't listen to people." How many times had Mom told her that? Always it made Nella angry, because how could you help listening? Now some mash-up of her mother and Sister Rosa sprang from her own lips. "People will say anything. It doesn't have to be true or even make sense. You know about sticks and stones, right? Sal, listen." When Nella looped her other arm around him, he actually let her. But then she couldn't think of anything more to say.

NELLA'S TURN NOT TO TELL
now

The sidewalk tables were empty. No one was buying lemon ice in Terraci's. The souvenir shop had a HALF PRICE SALE sign in the window. The lights were on at the bocce court, but no one was playing. The landslide had swept through and left a ghost town.

A small scissors snipped at Nella's heart. She'd hoped Sam would call her. Or maybe even come over. Probably she wasn't a good enough kisser. Probably after they said good-bye he smacked his forehead and wondered what he was thinking, kissing a girl with size-ten shoes and a thing for hedgehogs. Snip snip, went the scissors. Hearts really did have strings.

Nella should have been feeding Mr. T, but instead she lingered in the shadows of the bocce court. Overhead, a plastic bag crinkled in the branches of a tree.

Across the street, a girl was climbing the hill. A girl with a hat pulled low, despite the heat. Head down, she walked quickly.

Angela.

The cemetery gates got locked at five thirty, but every neighborhood kid knew how to sneak in. Nella had never tried it, out of loyalty to Dad, whose job was to clean up the empty beer cans and replace the yanked-out flowers. She followed Angela past the gates to a spot where the wall curved and at last became low enough to climb. Angela scrambled over. Nella hung back, watching. This was the wildest part of the cemetery, the closest it came to untamed. Angela hesitated a moment, getting her bearings, then set off down the slope. Nella scrambled to follow.

Along a faint footpath, up a shallow rise. Night was closing in, and Nella followed the golden gleam of hair poking out beneath the hat. Fireflies winked and something small scurried through the undergrowth. If Nella had believed in ghosts, she'd be scared by now.

It wasn't long before she knew where Angela was going.

Another curve in the path, and there, there she was.

Marie, reaching for the unreachable. It had been forever since the two of them brought her presents and wished she would speak to them. A twig crunched beneath Nella's foot, and Angela spun around. For a moment, her face lit up with happiness.

But then she yanked off the knit hat, and her hair spilled over her shoulders in a wavy tangle. So much hair, golden and shiny, a princess's hair. It should be beautiful— it was beautiful—but it was all wrong. Her braids! Where were Angela's neat braids?

"I told you to leave me alone!"

Nella gripped the back of the curved stone bench. She could feel the day's warmth still trapped inside.

"Promise not to tell anyone you saw me here," Angela said then.

"But why?"

"Just promise!"

"Okay."

How many times had they promised each other things? Big things, little things, important or silly things. They used to confide every secret, good and bad. The dusk nibbled away at Angela. Her hair was like this part of the cemetery—wild, uncared for. Lonesome. Lonesome hair.

"Since you were dumb enough to follow me"—Angela stuffed the hat in her pocket. Her hands clasped and unclasped, like they were having a fight—"I'll tell you. I did go see Anthony. We talked through a glass thing. I wasn't allowed to touch him."

"That's so mean."

Angela chewed her lip.

"How is he? Sorry, talk about dumb! He must be terrible."

"He told me what happened that night."

Did Nella want to hear this? She didn't know.

"He said . . . he said the baby was crying so loud. It filled up his ears. It filled up the whole world." Angela's hands grew still. "When I was little, he always came when I cried. Papa would be gone and she wouldn't pay attention, but Anthony . . . he was always right there. He's still that way. I hate to cry in front of him, because he gets so upset."

Nella gripped the back of the bench.

"He heard the baby crying and Mrs. Manzini screaming and . . . and he lost it. He said it was like somebody else took over, and all he could think was he had to save them. He heard Papa's voice telling him he wasn't a man and . . ." Angela looked into Nella's eyes. "He wouldn't tell me where he got the gun. He said don't worry, it would be all right."

He always said that.

"My father wouldn't talk to Anthony. He waited outside in the car."

"He should have! Anthony needs him."

Angela gave a small, startling snort.

"Do you know what paranoid is?"

"Umm . . . scared?"

"Times a million. It's being scared of things you can't see."

"You mean . . . like hell?"

"Worse."

"Worse than hell?"

Angela began picking pebbles off the back of the bench. The pebbles Nella had set there one by one over the years.

"My father talks to people who aren't there. Ghosts or demons." One by one, she dropped the pebbles into her palm. "Since they put Anthony in jail . . . I don't know if Papa ever sleeps."

"Ghosts?"

"He can't stop thinking about the people he saw die." She was dropping the pebbles faster now. Some missed and hit the ground. "It all comes back over him, and it's like he's right there again. He sees and hears and smells everything, even the blood gurgling in his buddy's throat."

A memory engulfed Nella: lying in their sleeping bags on Nella's bedroom floor. Angela whispering, *My father killed people. He watched his best friend die.* A terrible taste flooding her mouth. Pulling her own sleeping bag tight around her, so that no part of her touched Angela.

Time spun. It twisted and collapsed into a thin, transparent disk.

"He's been dead five years, and my father still hears that sound."

The gathering darkness smudged the edges of things. It softened Marie's face, so it looked like the stone was giving way, like she was turning real. Nella pressed her feet flat against the ground. There were no such things as ghosts.

"He can't stop wondering why he got to live and those others didn't."

Marie moved her hand. No she didn't! Nella shrank back against the bench.

Her father had a ghost too.

"He's trapped, so he keeps going around and around. He can't go backward to change what happened, and he can't go forward to forget it, so he's stuck. Stuck in the same time, forever. Just like Sister says hell is."

Angela closed her fist over the pebbles. She took a step back.

"Since Anthony went to jail, he's worse. Anthony could talk him down, but now . . ."

With her fist, Angela pushed the hair away from her face, and that was when Nella realized: Anthony was the one who did her braids. She never could have done them

251

so neatly by herself. After their mother left, he must've taken over. No wonder Angela had always worn braids, even though she knew they were dorky. Nella could see Anthony's quick, sure fingers spinning gold. She could feel them brush her own cheek.

"Anthony meant to do the right thing," she said.

Angela rattled the pebbles like dice.

"It's too late to talk about that."

Too late. Those were the ugliest words. The cruelest words. Time's worst trick of all.

"My father hid his gun. It's not in the case where he always kept it."

The breath went out of Nella.

"I asked him where it was and he said never mind."

This was too big. This was too much.

"You can't stay there. What if he . . . Call your aunt in Pittsburgh! Make her come get you."

Just like that, Angela hurled the pebbles. They hit Nella's cheeks and forehead, stinging. *Bullets,* Nella thought. Stumbling, she bumped against Marie.

"How can you say that?" Angela cried. "You think I'd leave Anthony? He took care of me and watched out for me my whole life. He loves me more than anybody. He loved me when nobody else did."

"But . . . your father doesn't know what he's doing. You

said so yourself—he doesn't always know where he is. He could hurt you!"

"He won't."

"How do you know?"

Angela was one of the fierce warrior angels, the ones who grasped shining swords.

"You can't tell anyone. If you do, they might put my father in the hospital or who knows what, and then where will I go? If they make me go someplace else, who will Anthony have? Who'll be here for him then?"

"But . . ." This wasn't right. Nella knew it.

"I can't leave Anthony. If anybody knows that, it's you." She stepped closer. "You followed me. You made me tell you. Now you have to keep it secret."

How could Nella do that?

"You owe me. You know you do."

"All right," whispered Nella.

Angela grabbed Nella's hand. Nella thought she'd make her pinkie swear, but instead she curled it around Marie's hand, then covered it with her own.

"Swear on Marie."

"I swear."

Angela turned and ran.

What did Nella just do? Did she stick by her secret sister, or betray her more deeply than ever before?

What the Statue of Jeptha A. Stone Would Say if Only, if Only It Could

Blame it on my foolish bird. Her bright wings. Her happy, jumbled song. The way she flies, as if the air were liquid and she a rolling vessel, steering home. To me.

Tonight, a child leaned against me and wept. I recognized her, from an autumn afternoon years ago.

My stone heart stirred.

Ow.

Hark unto me, Jeptha A. Stone: Coming to life is painful.

How I yearned to speak to her! What I would have given to say one word of comfort. To tell her she was not alone.

You mortals who still draw breath. You who can yet speak. Do you have any idea what power you possess?

Instead, I had to watch her walk away in the dark. My heart ached with fear.

Yet appearances often deceive. Perhaps she is stronger than she looks.

I, Jeptha A. Stone, pray it is so.

MI RICORDO
now

Nella got up early the next day, but Dad was already on the porch, drinking coffee. The sun still hadn't reached the top of the cemetery wall, and the moss at the base looked like black velvet. A yellow-flecked bird rode the breeze like an invisible roller coaster.

People in some religions, Nella knew, believed in reincarnation, where a spirit slipped free from a dying creature to live in a new one. She of course believed in an immortal soul that went to heaven or hell. But watching the bird disappear over the cemetery wall, for a moment she let herself pretend it was the spirit of someone buried there, set free to fly in the blue summer air.

"You're up early," Dad said.

"I had bad dreams."

"You and me both. Want to tell?"

She shook her head.

"Me either." He drained his mug and stood up. "It's going to be another scorcher. We're using so much water this summer, we . . ." He stopped, looking at her. "What?"

"Nothing. I mean. Dad? Do you believe in fate? Or do you think we get to choose how our lives turn out?"

Dad whistled under his breath. Just that second, the sun glided up over the stone wall. He squinted, like he was trying to see the answer, and now Nella was embarrassed.

"Never mind," she said. "It's just another one of my dumb questions."

"Just because I don't know the answer doesn't mean it's dumb. It probably means the opposite."

She watched him walk down the street. The secret Angela made her swear to—it beat up inside her, struggling to get out. Nella could feel its beak, its claws, its panicky wings. How could she keep it trapped in there? It was tearing away, desperate to get out.

Dad walked with his head down. Secrets. You thought you were keeping them, but maybe they were keeping you.

He was almost to the corner when Nella realized he'd forgotten his lunch. She grabbed it out of the refrigerator—Mom always made it for him the night before—and dashed after him.

"It's so frustrating." The nursing aide acted as if Nonni was deaf. Or even more insulting, as if she couldn't comprehend. "She won't do her therapy. Not physical, not occupational, not speech." The aide counted off Nonni's sins on her fingers, then heaved a dramatic, put-upon sigh. "There's only so much we can do with a patient who won't cooperate."

When the aide turned her back, Nella pressed her hand, thumb tucked in, against her nose. The sign for *drop dead*. The corner of Nonni's mouth quirked up. A glimpse of old, awful Nonni! Nella got excited.

"I won't tell Dad what a bad report you got," she promised her great-grandmother.

Nonni put a finger to her lips. "No Daaaa."

Nella almost told her, *Dad, say Dad,* the way she did with Vinny.

Nonni plucked at her blanket's loose threads. Nella was not supposed to upset her. But she was suddenly sick to death of bland small talk.

"Dad told me about how you visited him every Sunday while he was in jail," she blurted out. "Did you have to talk through glass?"

Nonni didn't seem surprised that Nella knew about Dad. Maybe she thought Nella always knew. Nonni never stopped loving him, so it made sense she'd think Nella never did either.

"He said after PopPop died, you had to take three buses, but you never missed. He said you beaned some guy who bad-mouthed him, right in church."

Nonni laughed. And it was wonderful, because it was her same, deep, clear laugh, bubbling up from deep in the Nonni-well. Her laugh had outwitted the stroke.

"You stood up for Dad. He says he couldn't have made it without you."

"Gaaa." Now Nonni scowled. Her eyes snapped. "Garr."

This was the first real conversation they'd had since the stroke.

"Mi ricordo," Nonni said. Or didn't say, really, but somehow Nella knew it was what she'd say if only she could. *I remember.*

But then, just as Dad had warned, Nonni looked worn out. The fireworks faded. Her eyes slowly closed.

CHUTES AND LADDERS
then

The year they were six, Nella and Angela developed a Chutes and Ladders obsession. They played every chance they got. They always hoped to land on the square with the girl helping the injured boy. Land there and you shot up an enormous ladder, almost to the top of the board. Worst was the kids stealing cookies. Hit that square and you slid all the way back to where you started.

One afternoon Angela landed on the lucky square. Instead of shouting for joy and rocketing up the ladder, she plucked her game piece and dropped it back in the box.

"This game is dumb," she said.

Nella couldn't believe it. To her, games were only dumb when she lost.

"Just because you do something good doesn't mean you get a reward," Angela said.

Nella couldn't believe this either.

"Yes it does! Good people win and bad people lose."

"Not always."

"Anyway, you're going to win! How can you quit?"

But once Angela made her mind up about something, she wouldn't budge. It drove Nella crazy.

(Years later, it would make all the difference.)

JAMES GARFIELD MIDDLE SCHOOL
now

That night, Nella watched the news. She Googled Anthony and D'Lon. Other stories had taken their place. This should have been a relief, but instead it made her furious. The media had gotten bored and tossed them aside.

But D'Lon was still dead. His boys had no father.

Anthony was still in jail. And Angela had no one.

Unless you counted Nella.

"Nella." Mom came up behind her as she sat at the computer. "I haven't checked my email for a while, but I did today, and there was one from the school district." As soon as she put her hand on Nella's shoulder, Nella knew

261

what she was going to say. "Getting into a magnet school was very competitive this year. More competitive than ever before. They only took . . . I forget. Some tiny percent."

It wasn't as if Nella ever expected to get in. Not as if she believed in magic.

"I know you tried your best. And I know you're going to succeed, no matter what. You're so . . ."

"It's okay, Mom." Nella jumped up. "You don't have to say all that."

Mom bit her lip. Some dried oatmeal—Nella hoped it was oatmeal—clumped the tip of her hair.

"You'll be all right at James Garfield." Her mother was trying to convince herself as well as Nella. "The teachers will love you. Some of the other St. A kids will be there, and you can all stick together. It won't be so bad. Dad will drive you so you don't have to take the—"

"I said it's okay, Mom."

"Maybe next year we'll figure out how to swing St. Moloc's." The V between her eyes was an arrow pointing toward her heart. "More than anything, Dad and I want you to have the best education. The best everything, Nella."

"I know," Nella said. "I know, Mom."

Nella tucked the stolen scarf into her pocket. The house across the street from Nonni's was quiet, no one in sight. She slipped up onto the porch and stood for a moment, pretending she lived here. She played an instrument, she had drawers full of silky things, and an infinitesimally cute boy was in love with her. What she yearned for and what she had were one and the same.

That, Nella thought—that had to be the definition of happiness.

She pulled the scarf from her pocket, stuffed it in the mailbox, and ran back down the steps.

It wasn't till she was on her way to take care of Mr. T that she thought, *Clem must have gotten an email too.* Given how Mr. and Mrs. Patchett were Velcroed to their phones, Clem had read her news a long time ago.

But she hadn't said a word.

Was that good or bad?

Bad. Bad for sure.

She turned up the walk to Clem's front door.

"Where were you last night?"

She tripped and hit the dirt. Sam Ferraro crouched beside her.

"What?" She blinked at him.

"I waited for you here."

Her head spun. And not from falling. "You did?"

"For a century. See this? It's gray hair."

A boy waited for her. This boy. Waited and waited. For *her.*

"Why didn't you come?" he asked.

"I . . . I can't tell you."

He thought she was teasing. She pretended she was.

Nella would have happily lain there on the ground forever, except now Sam took her hand and pulled her up.

Inside, they fed Mr. T, then sat on the enormous leather couch. Nella told him she was going to Garfield Middle for sure. Sam didn't look as pleased as she hoped. He said he was getting really nervous about that school. The kids would think he was an uncool white punk. They'd stuff him in a locker or drop him off the bleachers headfirst.

"No they won't."

"They will when they find out I'm from this neighborhood. After what happened."

Nella leaned back. She wondered if he was right.

"But that's too messed up," she said. "It's judging us without knowing us."

"You can explain that to them while they're beating me up."

"Everyone here isn't the same. We don't all think alike—we're all different. Am I like Victoria? Or Nonni? Please God, no." She sat up straighter. "So it's a big mistake for us to think they're all alike. The Garfield kids." This was such a simple, obvious fact, why hadn't Nella ever realized it before? Really realized it? She felt excited, even hopeful, as if she'd figured out something big, and now maybe she'd start to understand other important things too. "I mean, we need to give each other a chance. Get to know each other, one by one. Get to know each other period. Because we don't, not at all. We don't know the first thing about each other." *Nulla*, that's what they knew. Nothing.

"So you're not scared about going there?"

Nella slid down on the couch. She regarded her ocean-liner feet.

"I'm so scared I could die."

"You know what I think?" Sam said all of a sudden. "I think God's not really watching over us."

"What?" She sat back up.

"He's more like *Sorry, guys. I created you but now I'm busy. Good luck.*"

"I don't believe that for a minute."

"It just makes sense," Sam said. "How can He keep track of billions of people?"

"He's God!"

"Hmm."

"Sister Rosa told me the reason God made so many people is so we can help each other."

"See what I mean?" Sam grinned. "God's trying to get off the hook."

"Or maybe He just really trusts us to do what's right."

"Wow," said Sam. "You have an answer for everything."

At the street corner, tucked in the shadows of the bocce court, they kissed again. Nella hoped she was getting better at it.

A SMALL, PURE BELL
now

This summer, Salvatore had developed his own secret, separate life. He knew things about the neighborhood before any of the rest of them. Nella was getting ready to take Vinny for a walk when he ran up the driveway.

"Come see what they did!"

The front window of Angela's house was smashed. Cracks radiated out from a jagged hole like in that poster of Clem's, the one of a nebula, a doomed, exploding star. Shards of glass lay on the lawn.

"They did it last night." Salvatore's eyes were round.

"Who?" One of the protesters, she thought. That's why

they weren't here today.

"Everyone says Kenny Lombardo. Drunk out of his mind."

Kenny Lombardo! He was from *here*.

Now Victoria and Kimmy appeared.

"Oh my God," said Victoria.

"Oh my God," said Kimmy.

"That idiot Kenny!" Victoria's hand flew to her hip. "What a loser. I bet he was trying to impress his loser girlfriend."

"I heard him saying the DeMarcos have a curse on them and they should get out of town," said Kimmy.

"I'm surprised the newspeople aren't here." Victoria looked around, disappointed. "And where are the cops?"

"They came," said Salvatore. "But there's no witnesses."

"Oh sure." Victoria gave a halfhearted hair flip. "Like loser Kenny goes anyplace without his loser posse? But they'll never talk."

Bored, she and Kimmy wandered away.

It looked like a Halloween haunted house now. An abandoned poster, STOP THE HATRED, lay near the steps.

"Nella," Salvatore said, "it's supposed to rain tonight." Before she could answer, he darted across the grass.

"What are you doing?" Nella struggled to maneuver the balky stroller but banged into the bumper of a parked car.

"We need to fix the window," Sal said. "She'll get wet."

The front door opened. Angela stepped outside. Barefoot.

"Salvatore Sabatini!" she scolded. "Don't touch that glass! Do you want to cut yourself?"

Obediently he dropped the piece of glass. He looked ready to hug her, then slid his hands into his pockets.

"You look different," he said quietly.

Vinny was trying to climb out of the stroller. Angela crossed the grass and touched a finger to the tip of his nose.

"Hey you," she whispered when he grabbed it. "Hey, Vin-vin."

"You want me to fix the hole?" Salvatore asked. "It's supposed to rain."

"Don't worry. We'll fix it. Don't worry." She darted a look back at the house. "Get going now. Shoo before you cut yourself." But Vinny still gripped her finger, and she didn't move.

From inside came the sound of something heavy falling. A groan, followed by rasping sounds, the kind of sounds Nonni made when she had her stroke.

"What's that?" Salvatore grabbed her other hand.

"Nothing. Nothing, you silly."

"Blood!" yelled Salvatore. "You're bleeding!"

"Angela!"

Three syllables, pure and clear, like a small, perfect bell

ringing for the first time. Arms outstretched, Vinny spoke.

"Angela!"

Nella and Angela gaped at each other. Their faces were astonished mirrors.

"Did you hear that?"

"Yes!"

They crushed Vinny between them. They made a Vinny sandwich.

"Come home with us," begged Salvatore. "Mom has Band-Aids."

Angela wanted to—her face was full of wanting to. But now she pulled down that mask, turning her face blank as a statue.

"I'll be fine," she said. "Right, Nella? Tell Sal I've got Band-Aids and I'll be fine."

Nella nodded, mute as a statue.

It must be so terrible to be a statue.

Angela disappeared inside. The deadbolt clicked into place. All went quiet. Quiet as a tomb.

"Angela?" called Vinny. "Angela!"

DO-OVER

now

"Listen to this one, Nonni. *What did the finger say to the thumb? I'm in glove with you.*"

Nella broke the Laffy Taffy into pieces. Nonni sucked noisily.

"Guess what? Vinny said *Angela*. He said it clear as anything."

Interest flickered in her eyes. "Aaa-eee."

"What?" asked Nella, though she knew exactly what her great-grandmother had just said.

"Aaa-o-eee."

"Anthony."

Nonni nodded. She sat up straighter, giving Nella her full attention.

"Anthony's her big brother," Nella said, stalling. She was forbidden to talk about this. "He . . . she . . ."

Nonni regarded Nella like she was the one with brain damage. *Spit it out,* said her face. And now Nella couldn't help herself. She wanted to tell, needed to tell, had to tell.

"He's in serious trouble, Nonni. He's in jail."

Nonni got a distant look, like someone trying to remember a dream. After a long moment, she nodded again.

"Eye-oh."

"You know?"

Another nod.

"You saw it on the TV that morning. We thought you forgot."

Nonni shook her head so hard, the veins in her neck stood out. Oh no. She wasn't having another stroke, was she? Nella poured her a cup of water, but Nonni batted it away and it tumbled to the floor. She gripped the arms of her wheelchair and leaned forward like Vinny in his stroller, trying to go faster.

"Daaad." Her voice was a foghorn. "Daaad."

272

"Dead. I know. D'Lon Andrews is dead. *Morto*. Nonni, are you all right?"

Nonni shook her head, furious. No! No, she was not all right, or no, Nella was wrong? Wrong as always?

"Daad," she repeated. Her face took on a strange brightness, and Nella realized she'd begun to cry. Tears ran down her cheeks and pooled in her wrinkles. Never, ever had she seen her great-grandmother cry. Something inside Nella came unhinged. It swung loose like the door to an abandoned house.

"Dad," she said softly. "It made you remember what happened to Dad."

Nonni fell back in her chair. The tears dropped onto her threadbare black-widow sweater. Maybe, Nella thought, maybe the stroke wasn't all my fault. Maybe the shock of what happened to Anthony was part of it. He reminded Nonni of Dad at the same age, and her heart broke all over again.

It was impossible for time to go backward. But so many things that once seemed impossible had turned out not to be. What if Nella got things wrong, but now she had a chance to get them right? A do-over. She touched her great-grandmother's sleeve.

"I meant to come see you the night before, but I was too late. I'm sorry."

Nonni kept shaking her head.

No no no. No she didn't forgive Nella, or no it didn't matter, or just no, no to the whole universe and everything in it? And then Nella had a terrible thought. It was so terrible, she tried to push it away, but it roared back with all the fierce, stubborn power of Nonni herself.

"You're not giving up, are you, Nonni?"

Nonni curled her hand and struck her chest. It was what the old ladies did at Mass when they prayed the confiteor. *By my fault, by my fault, by my most grievous fault,* they said, knocking their breasts with their bony fists. Now Nella really felt scared.

"You can't! No!" She pressed her hand to her heart. *No,* it said with each beat. *No no no,* it protested. "Nonni, I know this is hard, it stinks, it bites—but you can get better. The doctors say."

Nonni made a disgusted sound. Nella didn't know what to do, how to convince her. Desperate, she unwrapped another taffy.

"How do you get a peanut to laugh?" she read. *"You crack it up."*

The tears were still running down Nonni's face, and she darted out her tongue to lick one away. A little beam of sunlight pushed its way through the blinds. It fell across the bed, lit up a corner of this sorry room.

"Nonni, the doctors say you're lucky." Nella set the

box of tissues in her great-grandmother's lap. "Maybe there's no such thing as luck, or fate, or divine mercy, or I don't know, but you're here. Here you are, alive. And if you try, things will get better. If you fight. Who's a better fighter than you? Nobody!"

Nonni clutched at her sweater. Nella wanted to tell her that if she died, part of Dad would too. But making Nonni feel guilty wasn't fair or right.

"The way you fought for Dad—you saved him, Nonni. In a way you saved our whole family. Now you have to fight like that again. Only this time for your own self."

Nonni glared. *Don't tell me what to do, you terrible girl.* But something had shifted. Nonni was listening.

"Okay, you don't have to fight. You can cave. It's up to you. You have free will, after all."

Nonni growled. Nonni scowled. Nella plucked a tissue and tried to touch her dripping nose, but Nonni grabbed it and did it herself.

"See?" said Nella, and her great-grandmother gave a crooked grimace. She reached for another piece of Laffy Taffy, but somehow her hand instead came to rest on top of Nella's, and stayed there.

Sam had to go visit his cousins, so Nella took care of Mr. T alone. Clem was due back in just a few days, but instead of

275

happy, Nella was nervous. She'd lost track of when they'd last talked. So much had changed since Clem left, it was easy to imagine that Clem would be different too.

Outside, it was raining, just as Salvatore predicted. Who knew little brothers could grow up? Who knew they wouldn't always remain booger-eating, head-butting creatures? Witness: tonight at supper, he was wearing cologne. Approximately half a gallon. The smell was over-powering. One thing for sure: he was going to need some grooming tips.

A stiff breeze flapped Mama Gemma's awning. Why was it so cold? What was Mother Nature thinking? Tired and wet, all Nella wanted was to be inside. But just as she reached her own corner, another brother's voice sang in her ear, pure as the song of a yellow-flecked bird.

Angela. An-gel-a!

Vinny's voice took her by the hand. It tugged her past her own street, all the way to Angela's house. Somebody had taped a square of cardboard over the hole. The wind picked at it, trying to get in. The rain drummed on the roof.

Nella remembered summer mornings when a brother would open the front door and find Angela already there, waiting for the family to wake up. By the time Nella came downstairs Angela would be nestled on the couch, reading to them, or in the kitchen pouring milk on their cereal.

Nella tiptoed across the strip of grass and tried to stick the corner of cardboard back down.

Angela always seemed like the weakling, and Nella the strong one. But maybe this was another thing Nella got wrong.

She ran all the way home, like something was chasing her.

What the Statue of
Jeptha A. Stone
Would Say if It Could

S he sits upon her nest rain or shine.
And I thought I was dignified.

THE COUNTDOWN BEGINS
now

C lem pulled clothes out of her suitcase and tossed them into drawers. So far she hadn't sat down once. Her nose had new freckles, and her new bandanna was printed with whales. Her energy level had gone from extremely high to dangerously frenetic.

"And another crazy thing," she was saying. "Great white sharks! Half the people warn you not to swim when seals are in the area, because they attract sharks. The other half says *only* swim when seals are in the area, because that means there *aren't* any sharks."

"So which did you do?" Nella asked.

"I boogie boarded every day no matter what." She flung flip-flops in the vicinity of her closet. "Also I became a vegetarian, after seeing one too many lobsters boiled alive. Not to mention heartless adults sucking down raw oysters."

"But you adore cheeseburgers."

"I know." Clem sounded sad.

Clem! Nella had missed her even more than she knew. But Clem felt nervous too, Nella could tell. That's why she wouldn't sit down, wouldn't quit talking so fast and so loud. Mr. T gave a sleepy squeak.

"He's dreaming," said Nella. "That's his dreaming sound."

"I missed my guy." Clem rushed over to the cage and plunged in both hands. A huff and a puff and she was doing jazz hands. "Zoinks! Vicious hedgehog attack!" She stuck her fingers in her mouth and immediately yanked them back out. "Aack, aack! Including the dreaded green poop!"

She rushed to the bathroom. Nella murmured hedgehog words of comfort, and Mr. Tiggywinkle grunted in reply. Nella resolved not to tell Clem about Sam. Clem would tease and Nella wouldn't be able to stand it.

The second Clem reappeared, her attacked hand wrapped in a towel, Nella cried, "Sam Ferraro kissed me."

"*What?*"

"Right here in your room."

"Shut up!"

"And by the bocce court, too."

Clem staggered backward. She keeled over onto the bed in her chopped-down-tree imitation.

"I told you he was in like with you," she said. Then repeated it again and again, till Nella was forced to pillow-clobber her. Clem fought back with super-pillow-fighting powers. It was a battle to the death. Neither one would surrender, till finally they were both on the floor, limp and gasping and staring up at the glow-in-the-dark galaxy. Just like always. Everything was once more Right Between Them. P2F2. Past Present Future Friends.

Then her best friend sat up.

"I got into Charles Chestnutt Magnet School. The science one. I think I'm going to go."

Nella didn't move. She focused on Saturn. "You think?"

"I am. I'm going. My parents said it was up to me, and I chose."

Now Nella studied a plastic comet. Glow-in-the-dark galaxies looked incredibly dumb in the daytime.

"I didn't get to choose. Big surprise."

Clem ran her hand through her hair. Her glasses sat crooked on her nose. "Standardized tests are notoriously poor indicators of intelligence."

"It's okay. I mean, congratulations. I know that's what you really wanted."

"We'll still be together all the rest of the time! School's just an incidental part of our friendship."

"Right."

Clem hunted up her bandanna and slowly tied it back on. Nella could practically hear the unsaid thoughts whirring around in her head. But what Clem said next was a surprise.

"How's Angela?"

That was when Nella understood: without being conscious of it, she'd been saving up to tell Clem. Clem who was so smart, such a better thinker than she was. Clem would know what to do. Nella had been counting on it. Now, telling her felt impossible.

"When Angela and I were little, we called each other secret sisters. Because we both really wanted a sister. And because . . . well. We kept so many secrets together."

Clem got that mischievous look Nella usually loved. "Tell me one."

"They're *secrets*!"

"Fine!" Clem looked startled. "Pardon me!"

"I better go."

At the door, Clem said, "The countdown has begun." When Nella looked baffled, she shook her head sadly. "You forgot again."

"No I didn't! What?"

"The leap second!"

"Oh. Right."

"The correct response is not *Oh. Right.* It's *It's not too late. We are time sisters. Masters of the hour. Commanders of the minute and lords of the leap second!*"

"Oh. Right. I mean . . ."

They were having trouble looking at each other. It was time for Nella to go.

That night Dad grilled hamburgers, and they ate outside at the picnic table. Seconds and minutes flew by, and the Sabatinis took no notice whatsoever. Until Mom started to cut Vinny's meat up for him, and he shook his head.

"Bun," he said.

"He said he wants a bun," Bobby automatically translated. "Hey, wait a minute!"

Mom quickly put a burger on a bun and handed it to Vinny. Everyone watched as he took a big bite.

"Good," he said.

A moment of stunned silence before they all burst into cheers. Vinny cheered too, waving his arms till the burger flew out of the bun and landed in the grass. Mom smothered him with kisses.

"For the love of God," said Dad with a grin.

"I told you he could talk," Bobby said.

Later Vinny said "moon." He pointed at a firefly and said "wi-fi." It was as if he'd crossed over from one land to another, and was at last adopting the language and customs. Mom took this as a beacon of hope. For the first time in weeks, she looked as happy and beautiful as she used to.

SEASHELL, AGAIN
now

Nella still had most of the hundred dollars she got for
hedgehog sitting. New clothes for Garfield Middle
would gobble that up, but she saved five dollars to put in
the "bale" jar. Except when she got to Franny's, the jar
wasn't there.

No one behind the counter knew where it was. Worse,
nobody seemed to have noticed it was gone.

Nella went back outside and sat at a sidewalk table.
Clem was supposed to meet her here, but fifteen min-
utes (how many seconds?) went by and she didn't appear.
Nella started to feel like the jar. Lost, and nobody noticed.

Pigeons pecked at the sidewalk crumbs and each other.

Just as Nella was telling herself Clem completely forgot, she appeared, arms flailing and flannel shirt flapping.

"Sorry sorry sorry!" She flung herself into a chair, annoying the pigeons. "Glacially paced school orientation. Guess what? We have to wear uniforms! So much for becoming a fashion icon."

Clem wouldn't care if they made her wear a burlap sack like the fig tree—she was only pretending for Nella's sake. And even though they had an oath against pretending with each other, it felt nice. It felt like a token of friendship, and Nella accepted. Clem was pulling pens and notebooks out of her cargo pants pockets. Nella got a whiff of grapefruit. Clem! Infinitely hopeful and excited about the world and its million trillion wonders.

If any single person in this world was the opposite of Angela, it was Clem.

"Did I ever actually explain how it all works? There's something called Earth's Master Clock. And every midnight Universal time, which is eight P.M. our time in the summer, it goes from 23:59:59 to 00:00:00. The night of the Leap Second, though, they'll make it go to 23:59:60 instead. Thus giving the world the gift of a free second."

"Okay."

"So here's my idea. Patch used to be into model rockets,

and he still has a couple. They shoot up like three hundred feet! We go up on my roof. We have a countdown, and at the exact moment of the extra second—" She stopped. "Uh-oh. You think it's a feeble idea."

"No! It's just . . . I mean, a rocket goes up and comes down and that's it. What's the point?"

"Okay." Clem folded her arms on the table. "What's your idea?"

"Shouldn't it be something more permanent? Like . . ." Like what? Clem was looking at her expectantly. "How about a plaque? *On This Spot Clementine Patchett and Penelope Sabatini Witnessed the Leap Second*?"

"I don't know." Clem frowned. "It sounds cemetery-like. Like *Here lies so and so, rest in peace*."

Why didn't Nella give this more thought? She didn't realize how much it meant to Clem. Why didn't she realize?

"You're right," Nella said. "A second is so *ephemeral*."

"Not as ephemeral as an attosecond." Clem tapped her pencil on the table. "That's the smallest unit of time we can measure. So far. One hundred attoseconds is to one second as one second is to three hundred million years."

"Right." Nella never used to say *right* so much, did she?

Clem did more pencil tapping, which made Nella more nervous. Suddenly everything seemed to hinge on this special second. How did that happen? It was so dumb. She almost gave a fake laugh but stopped herself in time. Clem found her fake laugh excruciating. Nella couldn't do anything right. At their feet, the pigeons grumbled and argued.

"I need more time to think about this," Nella said. "Time for time!" She couldn't help it. Out popped the fake laugh.

"You had weeks to think about it." Clem set her pencil down. Then she picked it up and slipped it into a pocket. "Why don't you just tell the truth? You think the whole thing is a waste of time."

"No I don't!"

The notebook disappeared into another pocket.

"I get it, Nell. It's okay." But Clem's voice said no it wasn't, not at all.

"You faker!"

"Me? You're the faker! You don't care about the leap second or anything else that's important to me!"

"Who chose to go to a magnet school? And leave me in the dust?"

"The dust with *Sam*!"

A woman passing on the sidewalk stopped to frown at them. "Girls," she said. "Don't fight!"

"We're not!" they said at the same time. Then shrank into their chairs.

"Yes we are," Clem whispered.

"I know," Nella whispered.

"Patch calls it clearing the air."

"It doesn't matter what you call it. Words are meaning-less."

Why did she say that? Why didn't she say let's make up? Nella knew it now for sure: Clem was going to ditch her. Soon she'd be among fellow geniuses and wonder how she could ever have been friends with clueless Nell. Clem wouldn't miss her at all. Spoiled rotten Clem!

Nella's insides started to crumble. She could feel bits and pieces of herself breaking off.

Maybe this was how Angela felt.

"Nell." Clem reached into another pocket and pulled out a shell shaped like an ear. It was dull on the outside and pearly on the inside. "I forgot to give you this."

Nella held the shell-ear to her human ear, and they were a perfect match. The sounds of the street faded away, and she heard breathing. Only not in and out. Just out—a breath long and never-ending, like the whole infinite universe releasing its secrets.

"I kept finding shells I knew you'd like. I collected about ten million, but I decided if it was going to be a meaningful gift, I had to choose. I had to choose one and dis-choose the rest."

"I really like it."

"I'm really glad."

Nella went back inside Franny's. She spent the five dollars she'd meant for the bail fund on lemon sodas and Chinese almond cookies, which to her tasted like sawdust but were Clem's all-time favorite. When she came back out, Clem wore a weird look.

"I was praying so hard you wouldn't ditch me," she said.

"You don't pray!"

"I know."

SPEAK
now

Early the next morning, a sound woke Nella. She thought it was Vinny crying, but when she checked, he was deep asleep, bottom in the air, fistful of blanket pressed to his cheek.

Sssh. Did she hear it again?

She went downstairs. Nobody. The front door stuck in the humidity, and she had to tug it open. When she stepped out onto the porch, the world was misted gray and silver. Maybe this was how it looked before God created humans.

The birds were singing so loud, it was like they were

trying to wake the dead.

Turning to go back inside, she noticed something dark in the dewy grass. A footprint? There was another one, and another. A trail leading away from the house.

Nothing on the porch looked out of place. The boys' baseball bats, the stroller, Dad's dusty boots. The chairs were lined up same as always, and their cushions, when she touched them, were cool and damp. Except. This one, the one closest to the door. When Nella touched it, it was warm, as if someone had sat on it just moments ago.

"We're so proud!" the aide warbled, wheeling Nonni back from therapy. "We really worked hard today!"

Nonni drew a finger across her throat, which made Nella want to shout *Hooray!*

She and the aide helped Nonni into bed for her afternoon nap. Nella didn't want to go home yet, so she clicked on the TV with no sound and watched a soap opera, where you could tell who was good and who was evil just by their hairstyles and makeup. If only real life was that simple. It'd be so much less confusing.

Her sleeping great-grandmother snorted.

Nella used to tell Marie secrets she didn't tell anyone else, even Angela. How she was afraid her father wouldn't go to heaven. How sometimes she wanted to do crazy random things, like shout curses or smash dishes. How just between the two of them, if she had to choose between being bad and being happy, she wasn't sure which she'd pick.

"I don't know what to do," she whispered now to her great-grandmother. Who lay so still, eyes closed. Who could be a statue. Nella whispered how Angela made her promise to keep silent. "But should I?" Her voice rose—she couldn't help it. "She never snitched on me, ever. I owe her. Her and Anthony both. But what if something bad happens? Something really bad could happen. All because I didn't tell."

On TV, a woman with makeup thick as cake frosting laughed a silent, villainous laugh. Nella tried to swallow around the hard thing in her throat. For once in her life, she had choices, and she didn't want them.

"I don't know what to do," she said.

Nonni's arm shot out and grabbed Nella's wrist. Nella's heart tried to leap out of her chest. Those knobby fingers dug into her skin with all their old, furious strength.

"You." Loud and clear. "Know."

"I do?"

Leaning closer, she saw herself reflected in her great-grandmother's dark, shining eyes. Was Nonni awake all this time? Or maybe she was still asleep, talking in her

sleep? When had Nonni ever told Nella she knew anything? She looked into Nonni's eyes, into her own face.

"What do I know, Nonni?"

"Amore."

Nonni released Nella and folded her hands on the
covers. Within moments she was really truly asleep. Nella
looked down at the red dents her great-grandmother had
left in her skin.

Love?

Back home, Mom was all upset. Dad was an hour late and
not answering his phone. Dad always answered his phone.

"Maybe it died," said Nella. "Or he left it in his truck."

But Mom was worried. All that dangerous machin-
ery, accidents just waiting to happen. Dad always took the
worst jobs for himself, mowing the steepest hills, clearing
brush in the most remote spots. The rest of the crew would
be gone by now, the gates locked, and if something had
happened there was nobody to know or help him.

Mom picked up Vinny, but he wouldn't cuddle. He
squirmed, and when she set him down, she looked ready to
cry. She hated empty arms. Nella saw it on her face: Mom,
who always expected the best, was imagining the worst.

"I'll walk up and see," Nella said.

"The gate's locked by now!"

"No problem."

Mom's eyebrows went up, but she was desperate. "Be careful."

Nella scrambled over the low spot in the cemetery wall. She listened for the telltale sound of a weed whacker or backhoe, but all she heard was birdsong, spilling from every bush and tree. This time of day, when no living humans were around, was the most beautiful of all. In the slanting light, the grass was Day-Glo green. The neatly trimmed bushes stood guard along the paths. She circled the pond, where a family of ducks glided, a mirror family below them.

On the way to the office she passed Jeptha A. Stone and stopped. What did he have in his lap? As she tried to see, a somehow familiar bird swooped through the air, whistling a merry tune. Tiny whistles, whistles no bigger than a newborn's fingernail, answered. Tiny beaks tweezered the air. Nella laughed.

"You're a bird nursery!" she told the monument. Which of course didn't answer. Which couldn't hear, let alone speak. Nella felt a stab to the heart— a sudden, unreasonable pity for stony old Mr. Stone.

The office was locked up for the day. Dad's truck was parked behind. His phone lay on the seat, just as she'd guessed. But where was he? Mom's anxiety infected Nella.

She walked faster. The cemetery was like a city, one small neighborhood after another. She climbed a hill, hurried back down. People had gotten lost on these twisting paths. They'd gotten locked in after closing. Once, a man visiting his wife's grave had a heart attack, and nobody found him till the next day.

Nella started to jog. She tried the doors of the chapel— locked. A couple of geese, those poop machines, hissed as she ran by. Doubling back, she passed Daffodil Hill, then dipped into a hollow where most of the names were familiar. Lombardo, Manzini, Sabatini.

"Hi, PopPop," she whispered as she jogged by.

Past two square stones with a smaller one beside it. The little one had a carving of a woolly lamb. BABY, it said.

Maybe that was why, she thought suddenly. Maybe her parents had so many kids because they knew, knew so well, how fragile life could be.

The back of her throat drew closer. Where was he?

Ahead, a grove of trees glowed silver in the late sun. An ATV was parked nearby. At last Nella saw him, kneeling in the grass. She thought he'd dropped something, but then an invisible hand tipped him forward, and his palms flattened against the ground. His head hung down. He didn't move.

"Dad!" She hurried to him. "Daddy! Are you okay?"

He jerked upright, face contorted. "Nella! What's wrong? Is—"

"We didn't know where you were! We were so worried."

He sat back on his legs, and his face relaxed. Now he looked embarrassed.

This was when Nella noticed the flowers. Pots and pots of them, crimson and white, royal purple and butter yellow. And butterflies. Flitting and dipping, dusky wings trembling. The silver tree branches netted the air, and the breeze, caught by the leaves, murmured a sound soft as a lullaby. Nella must have walked past this spot before but never paused to appreciate it. Cradled in the grass was a single polished stone. Kneeling down, she read the inscription:

MARIE PONZO, AGED 7 YEARS

BELOVED DAUGHTER AND SISTER

NOW ANGELS ARE YOUR PLAYMATES

She read it again, then turned to her father. He gave the barest nod.

A yellow butterfly drifted down to settle on the stone. Nella shook her head.

"But I already found her grave." She pointed. "Back on the woodland path, the girl lifting her arm."

"That was you?" Dad's eyebrows did a backbend.

"Those funny presents? The stones on the bench?"

Nella flushed. "Me and Angela. We felt sorry for her, because no one ever came to visit."

"There's a good reason for that. That grave's over a hundred years old. Anyone who knew that Marie is long dead too."

He had to be wrong. "Are you sure?"

Dad smiled. He knew every grave, every single one.

Marie was not Marie. Nella had believed something else untrue, believed it with all her heart.

She was wrong again.

"Nobody's forgotten Marie Ponzo," Dad told her. "Her family moved away after she died, but they come back. Her parents, her big brother. He's married. His wife comes too. Soon Marie's going to be an aunt."

"You've seen them?"

"A few times."

More butterflies dipped among the flowers. It was Butterfly Paradise.

"I tried to talk to them once, right after, but they refused. I wrote them a letter from prison, but I don't know if they got it. Anyway, they never answered." He looked up into the protective branches of the tree. EUROPEAN BEECH said its sign. "It's too late now. I'd never approach them here. People come here to try to find peace."

The bird choir sang and sang, trying to hold the night and darkness back as long as they could.

"Maybe they forgive you," Nella said. "In their hearts, even though they never said it."

"I'd like to think that. But I'll never know."

Words welled up inside Nella, clogged her throat. Silent, she and her father watched the shadows stretch across the grass and scrub the day's colors away.

"You and Angela did a kind, good thing, kiddo," Dad said then. "What do we know? Maybe that other Marie appreciates it, wherever she is. I don't think you can ever call kindness a mistake."

This was so like something Sister Rosa would say.

"We better go," Nella said. "Mom is really worried."

They climbed into Dad's ATV. As they passed Jeptha A. Stone's monument, a movement caught Nella's eye. A disturbance in the air. And then she saw something in the grass. A tiny flopping creature. The yellow-flecked bird swooped over it, crying.

"Dad, look!"

A baby bird, bug-eyed and naked, quivered at the statue's feet.

"It fell out of the nest!" Nella jumped from the cart. "Oh, Dad!"

"Hang on!" He sped away. Minutes later he was back

with a ladder, which he leaned against Jeptha A. Stone's broad shoulders. The mama went out of her mind, flapping and whistling and jumping up and down on the nest.

"We won't hurt him," Nella promised her.

But the baby looked so fragile, Nella was afraid to touch it. It was the purest, most innocent thing she'd ever seen. Gentle and Decisive, she told herself. Whispering in baby-bird, she slipped her fingers underneath and lifted it. She could feel its heart. Did birds have hearts? A tiny innocent heart in her hands.

Standing up, she carefully passed it to Dad. The mother bird dive-bombed his head as he reached toward the nest. Direct hit!

"Yikes!" he cried. Then, "Home sweet home."

The two of them hugged and high-fived. Nella thought she saw a tear in his eye, but that couldn't be. Dad never cried.

Just like Nonni.

As he folded up the ladder, Nella suddenly stood very still.

"Daddy. Did you hear that?"

"What?"

Nella shook her head. She'd lost her mind for sure. She could have sworn she heard a voice, a ghostly rumble of a voice, say *Thank you*.

What the Statue of Jeptha A. Stone Said

Thank you.

NOW NOW NOW

Then, just like that, everything inside her gave way.
    "Dad! Dad."

Inside Nella, everything was falling. It was a landslide in there.

"Bella?" Her father looked at her in alarm.

"I love you. I thought I didn't anymore but I was wrong, I was wrong again. You're the same, my same dad, and I still love you the same. I don't know what— I was so angry at you, and we didn't talk, then it got too hard to talk, then it seemed impossible, but all this time, really, inside me, I still . . ."

"Hush, hush now." He touched her cheek. His big hand, those work-rough fingers. "It's okay. It doesn't matter now. I love you too, Nella. With everything that's good in me, I'll always love you."

THE TRUE TURTLE GIRL
now

Clem got excited easily, but even for her, this was over the top. The sun was barely up when she called.

"I thought of the thing! The perfect quintessential thing! Are you ready?"

There was a thump and a pause.

"I dropped the phone! I'm spazzing out! So here's my idea. I borrow Patch's watch, the one that keeps perfect time even on mountain peaks and ocean bottoms? You and I both have cameras. We count down, and at the exact precise moment, we take each other's picture. We record exactly who we are at that momentous moment. It's brilliant, you have to agree. It's ephemeral and permanent at the same time."

"I never look good in pictures."

"Nell!"

"Just kidding! It's a genius idea. It's like . . . like we grab that extra second and store it up. We put time in a bottle."

Or something.

"Exactly!" Clem sounded relieved. "I was scared it would fail your dumbness test."

"No! Not at all! I can't wait." Nella meant it. She didn't care what they did. She'd do anything Clem wanted, just so long as they stayed friends.

That afternoon, Dad wouldn't let Nella come with him to visit Nonni. He told her she needed a day off. Mom shooed her out of the house.

"Go have some fun!" she said. "Go on!"

Like Nella was still a little kid. Like fun was waiting around every corner.

Speaking of corners, Sam and some other boys were hanging around on hers. Since Clem came back, Nella couldn't predict when she'd see him. He flashed a smile, then quickly turned away. No way he was letting anyone else know he liked her. If he even really did.

He does, said a voice inside her. *You know he does.*

It sounded like a new voice. It sounded authoritative, not her usual Voice of Feeble and Futile Questions.

You know, said this voice. This newly installed GPS.

You know what you know.

Nella went to Nonni's house to water the fig tree. The fruit was almost ripe, plump and velvety. Her mouth watered.

"Hey! Hey!"

Oh no. Turtle Girl was at the bottom of the steps. No escape.

"The old woman who lives here? Did something happen to her? We haven't seen her."

Thank goodness, she undoubtedly meant.

"She had a stroke," Nella said. The girl was wearing the scarf Nella snitched. Did she wonder how it found its way to her mailbox? Or did miracles like that happen to her all the time?

"That's awful!" Turtle Girl said. What an actress! She actually sounded sincere. "Is she going to be okay?"

Nella nodded. Suddenly, this was something else she knew. Nonni would get better.

"She's a pistol."

"She's my great-grandmother. She's old. Too old to change. She's awful on the outside, but—"

"You don't have to tell me." Turtle

Girl eased the instrument case off her back and onto the ground. She folded both arms on top. "*My* great-granny? You would not believe the stuff she says. Like, once I was sitting on the ground, and she gave me this lecture about how if my girl-parts got cold, I'd get a congestion and never be able to make babies."

Nella would have been embarrassed, except that the way the girl burst into sudden laughter was so contagious.

"She's your great-grandmother's evil twin. They've got the same frown."

The girl made such a ferocious face, Nella laughed again.

"Nonni likes listening to you play. She loves music. Though her taste is awful. Mario Lanza!"

"He was actually an amazing tenor." The girl slid her arms through the straps on her case and hefted it. "Can you tell her the Gypsy across the street sends get-well wishes?"

"I'm sorry she calls you that."

The girl shrugged, as much as a person wearing an enormous case could. "I should've come over and told her my *real* name. I'm Cara."

"I'm Nella."

"Ciao, Nella."

"Ciao."

She was nice. Big sister nice. Nella fingered a leaf of the fig tree. Another mistake she'd made. Cara wasn't the person she thought. Shredding the leaf, she wondered if that meant she wasn't the person Cara thought.

"Cara?" She ran to catch up.

Cara smiled, surprised.

"You know that vigil?" Nella asked. "I saw you there."

"Oh. Oh my God." Cara's face squinched up. "Did you see his two boys? They reminded me so much of my little cousins, it broke my heart! How could that guy do it? How can he live with himself?" She stopped walking, and her face changed. "Wait. Do you know him?"

"He's my friend's big brother."

Cara looked horrified. She started walking again, faster now, scarf fluttering.

"His name is Anthony."

"I know that."

"But that's all you know."

"It's plenty, thanks." Cara walked even faster.

Long as Nella's legs were, it was a struggle to keep up. Obviously Cara regretted being nice to someone who turned out to be friends with a murderer.

"He taught me how to tie my shoes. After their mother left them, every morning he braided his sister's hair."

Cara stopped on the edge of the railroad trestle's muck and slime. She looked Nella in the eye.

"What are you trying to tell me, Nella?"

"Just . . . you don't know him. Like I didn't know you before, so I was sure you were one of those snotty college kids who think they're better than us. But we have stuff in common. We both like mean old ladies."

Cara peered through the shadows to the scoop of light on the other side.

"You've got stuff in common with Anthony, too," Nella said. "He likes to make art, the same way you make music. Probably there are other things. So . . . so don't think you know who he is. That's all."

Cara pulled a shaky breath. Some seconds went by. Then some more.

"I don't know him," she said. "And I don't want to."

A big truck rumbled up the hill, and Nella felt the sidewalk beneath them shudder. The vibrations ran up from the ground through her belly and settled in her chest. Cara was still gazing toward the sunlight, but now she turned.

"But Nella," Cara said at last. "When your granny gets home, you two can come over and Tyler and I will play for you."

"Is that the guy with all the hair?"

"Yeah." She smiled. "He's pretty good on the keyboard."

"We'll come. Even if I have to drag her."

Nella watched Cara readjust the straps of her case and forge up the hill. When her scarf slipped off, she didn't notice. Nella ran to give it to her, but Cara said, "You know what? That'd look pretty on you."

Maybe it wasn't too late.

"Nonni was really upset today," said Dad when he got home. "You have any clue why?"

He'd never know unless Nella told him. She could get away with this if she wanted.

"I told her about Anthony."

"For the love of God! I can't believe it! How many times did I tell you?"

"Dad. She already knew. She remembered seeing it on TV."

"She was really worked up, Nella. Talking crazy nonsense! Something about money, and her basement, and . . ."

"You could understand her?"

"Some."

"That's kind of amazing, isn't it? That's progress, isn't it?"

"It would be if she made any sense. And when I told her to rest, she almost bit my head off!"

"Wow. Sounds more and more like Old Nonni."

Dad couldn't quite hide his smile. Things were different between them now. Not that they'd started having heart-to-heart talks. Not even that Dad talked to her much more than before. But things were different. They were saying things to each other again, with and without words.

LEAP
now

I n one second:
   A bird's heart beats 10 times.

Light travels 186,000 miles.

Four babies are born and two people die.

Nella and Clem would snap the photos that captured their friendship forever.

They were in Clem's room, practicing clicking their cameras lightning quick.

"Three two one—*click!*"

Mr. Patchett's watch swam on Clem's skinny wrist. It could calculate time to one hundredth of a second.

"Three two one—*click*!"

Nella's photos clipped off the top of Clem's head, or her chin, or her left ear.

"I'm not good under pressure," she lamented.

Clem talked about the many different ways humans had measured time. How long it took a candle to burn down, or water to drip into a bucket, or sand to fill a glass. People piled up stones and studied their shadows. They tracked a certain star as it moved across the sky. They were never satisfied, always trying to find a better way to pin it down.

"Einstein said that the only reason for time is so that everything doesn't happen at once," she said. "Ready? Three two one—*click*."

This time Nella's feet got tangled and she almost dropped the camera.

Clem's look was dubious. "Maybe we should just take selfies."

"No! No way!" Nella panicked. She needed to prove to Clem how serious she was about this. They had to do this *together*. "I'll get it right. I promise!"

Nella had brought her things for a sleepover. Mom was glad she was "having fun," and Nella hadn't tried to explain about the Leap Second. They ate an early dinner of Patchett Food—tofu with piles of nearly raw vegetables— and then they left to scout the neighborhood for the perfect photo location. They had about an hour, but every other minute Clem checked her father's watch.

The playground. The front steps of the church. An empty table outside Mama Gemma's. No place satisfied Clem, who kept whipping off her bandanna and tying it back on. Nella had no idea what they were looking for. Clouds were moving in, and though the sun wouldn't set for a while yet, the sky was gray and lifeless. It could have been any time at all.

"Clem, how did they decide to add the extra second tonight, instead of yesterday or tomorrow?"

"I told you. Cesium clocks."

"So they're exactly sure it's tonight?"

"Of course!" Now Clem's look grew suspicious. "Why? What are you thinking?"

"Nothing. Only . . . I feel bad for all the other, regular seconds. The ones that just pass into nothingness and never get to be special."

Clem pulled her glasses off. "Are you making fun?"

"Huh?" Nella re-panicked. Was she? "No! I'm just asking a question."

"Hmm." Clem cleaned her glasses with the hem of her T-shirt and carefully settled them back on her nose. "I haven't come across any research that says seconds have *feelings*. So I don't think we need to feel sorry for them."

Heat lightning flashed above the rooftops. Nella didn't like her neighborhood at night, when it mostly belonged to Invaders who came to drink and eat too much. Somebody had left an empty pizza box on the church steps. By now the school was well on its way to becoming the Heavenly Spa. In the school yard, two Dumpsters overflowed. St. Amphibalus gazed out on a pile of rubble. Nella looked up at the windows of their sixth-grade classroom. There were no such things as ghosts, but sometimes in the dark, eyes played tricks. A nun glided by, holding a book. A girl pressed her nose to the glass. The cemetery didn't spook Nella, but her abandoned school did.

"Not here," she said.

Out on the sidewalk, someone was hurrying in their direction, head down. Clem clutched Nella's arm. She hadn't seen Angela all summer and looked confused.

"Zoinks," she said.

Angela looked up, startled. "Nella!"

"Are you okay?"

"I don't know where he went." Angela looked around wildly, then pulled a piece of paper out of her pocket. "I shouldn't have left him. But he was drinking again and I couldn't stand it, so I went to see Marie."

Clem pivoted back and forth between them. Him? Marie? Nella saw the questions on her face.

"When I got home, he was gone. This was on the table."

It was one of Anthony's drawings—a portrait of Angela missing a front tooth. What was Mr. DeMarco doing with such an old drawing? Could he have saved it all these years? A note was scrawled across the back, the handwriting impossible to read. The only words Nella could make out were *I'm sorry.*

I'm sorry. The list of all the people Mr. DeMarco was furious at scrolled through her brain. The list was so long, her brain gave out.

His gun. He had a gun.

"He took the car. He shouldn't be driving." Angela looked around again, as if he might appear out of the air. "He hasn't left the house in weeks. I never thought he'd—"

"Who should I call?" Clem whipped out her phone. "Should I call my father?"

Angela jumped like she'd forgotten Clem was there.

"What? No, never mind!" She stuffed the note back in her pocket. "He'll be fine. I'm such a drama queen. What . . . what are you two doing out here, anyway?"

Clem hesitated, then explained the Leap Second. Angela pretended to be interested. She was such a bad liar, it was painful to watch. Clem didn't seem to notice. She pressed the light on her father's watch, and a circle of eerie green glowed.

"Do you want to come with us?" she asked. Which was, Nella knew, an enormous sacrifice on her part. Which was so generous and kind, it made Nella want to be friends with her forevermore.

Of course Angela said no.

"I . . . I have things to do." She darted Nella a look, and it was as if she put something in Nella's hand. A small stone. "Thanks anyway."

"Are you sure?" pressed Clem. "Are you sure you're okay?"

Angela was already walking away, waving, fake smiling. Nella's hand closed over the invisible thing it held.

"That was very strange," Clem said. "I cannot figure out that girl."

Thunder rumbled in the distance.

"We really need to decide." Clem tapped her father's watch. "Time is running out."

Angela was a small, pale person who grew paler and smaller as she walked away. In Nella's hand, the invisible thing began to pulse. It beat like an impossibly fragile heart.

"Clem, I don't think I can do this."

"Huh? "

"I should go with her."

"But . . ." Clem took off her glasses and put them back on. "But she said everything's all right. She said—"

"I'm really sorry. I know how much you—"

"You seriously want to?"

No, you don't, cried her heart. *Going after Angela is the last thing you want to do.*

"She needs me."

"So do I!" Clem's face crumpled into confusion and hurt. "You promised."

Stay, Nella's heart said. *That's what you want.*

But what if your heart wasn't the only voice you needed to listen to?

"Fine. It's your choice!" cried Clem, suddenly angry. This was it, the end of their friendship. "Go ahead. Do what you want. Go on!"

"I'm really really sorry."

Nella turned and started to run. For once, her feet skimmed the ground, sure and quick.

"Angela! Angela, wait!"

Her voice leaped out from somewhere impossibly deep inside. Like something that had been waiting a long time, it unfolded and stretched, reached and glimmered on the dark air.

YOU KNOW
now

How could they ever find him? By now he could be miles away.

Still, they searched every street, checked every parking lot. Nella walked ahead, their old pattern. In the rubble-strewn lot at the end of Sam's street, a bulky, dark shape lay in the weeds. Together, not breathing, they inched toward it.

An old mattress. A pile of rags.

They checked the alley behind Mama Gemma's. A huge rat scuttled out from a row of trash cans. It was dark now. If Dad knew Nella was out here instead of at Clem's, he'd have a fit.

Because he loves me, she thought. *Because he wants me to be safe.*

And then she thought, *All this time I was sure I was stronger than Angela. But maybe, maybe I was just safer.*

Somehow they circled back to the school yard. Clem was nowhere in sight. Clouds blotted out the stars. The air had a metallic smell. Without even thinking, they headed for St. Amphibalus and huddled, exhausted, at his feet.

The first drops of rain fell. Looking up, Nella saw those faithful, eyeball-less eyes were wet and shining. He was trying his best to keep them safe and dry, but he couldn't. The wind picked up, slanting the rain toward them, and now it seemed as if there wasn't a single dry, warm place left in all the world. Nella wanted to go home. She needed her family.

She was so lucky to have her family.

You know, said Nonni. *Love. You know love.*

"Angela, let's go to your house. Maybe he came back by now."

What the Statue of St. Amphibalus Would Say if It Could

God bless you, secret sisters! Be careful!

EVERY SINGLE SECOND
now

The driveway was empty. The house dark. Nobody was here.

In the distance, a dog gave one short, sharp bark. How long had they been searching? Nella had no idea, but she knew she'd missed the Leap Second. It had slipped by without her noticing, and now it was lost forever.

Nella felt sad, but relieved, too. It was over, and she didn't have to pretend to care about it anymore.

Angela put a hand on the doorknob. She drew a quick, choppy breath.

"Thanks for looking," she said. "I appreciate it."

It took Nella a moment to understand that Angela expected her to leave now. Well, why wouldn't she?

The rain pelted the cardboard, the dried-up grass, a cat skulking across the street. It hit Nella's cheeks and shoulders and washed everything together, and she heard Clem saying, *The only reason for time is so that everything doesn't happen at once.* How could anyone ever believe one second was more important than another? Every one mattered.

Like this one.

"I'm not leaving you," she told Angela.

Inside, the trash can was overflowing, and there was a bad smell. Nella had never seen so much as a fingerprint or scuff mark in this house. Angela got some not-exactly-clean towels and they rubbed their wet hair.

The ringing of the phone was loud as a shot. Angela crossed the kitchen and read the caller ID.

"Police," she whispered.

What the Statue of
Jeptha A. Stone
Wanted to Say More than Anything

When the nestling plummeted, my heart stopped.

Jep Stone, I told myself, *you no longer possess a corporal heart. You are deceived and deluded!*

My exquisitely carved ears refused to listen.

Yet no matter how desperate I was to rescue her baby, I could not move. Never in my 120 years have I felt more helpless.

Steady on, Jeptha, I admonished myself. *You are surrounded by departed souls. Death is your constant companion. This is a mere featherless bird!*

I could see its tiny heart beating beneath its skin.

I heard the rumble of a vehicle. The quiet, faithful man who cares for us all! If anyone could save the day, it was he.

Then, if ever, did I yearn to speak. Then, if ever, did I summon all my formidable strength and try.

Stop! Halt! Help us please!

She heard me. She looked up, her father's goodness shining in her eyes.

LEAP SECOND
now

"Yes. . . . Yes, I'm his only relative. . . ." Angela clutched the phone. "Could you say that again?"

Nella sat on the edge of the couch. The patched front window looked like a scabbed-over wound. She couldn't hear what the person on the other end was saying, only a flat monotone, the voice of someone used to giving bad news.

"Wait. Where?" Angela knuckled her forehead. "Is he—"

Nella closed her eyes.

"Which hospital?"

Oh no. No.

"Yes. . . . No, I'm not alone."

Nella opened her eyes to find Angela looking at her.

"Okay. Okay. I'll be there as soon as I can. Thank you." She clicked off. "He crashed the car. They took him to the VA Hospital."

All Nella could think was *Thank God*. Because if he was hurt, he couldn't hurt someone else.

It took a moment before she noticed how Angela had begun wildly rummaging through the kitchen junk drawer.

"Do you have some money I can borrow?" she asked over her shoulder.

"Money? What? Angela, is he okay?"

"He's not going to die, if that's what you mean." Now she pulled her father's jacket off a hook and went through the pockets.

"What are you doing?"

"They won't let me on the bus for free."

"The bus? This time of night? You'll wait a million years for one."

Angela ignored her. She opened the front door, and the rainy night gusted in.

"He crashed on D'Lon Andrews's street. They think he passed out. But when the police came, he fought them off." Angela put a hand up against the rain. "I bet he had a flashback. Nobody can reach him when that happens."

She stepped outside. It was raining harder, the kind

of rain that wets you to the skin in half a second. That old, familiar anger rose up inside Nella. Mr. DeMarco was drunk. He had a gun. Who knew what would have happened if he hadn't cracked up the car? He was a dangerous man, and he'd hurt Angela far too much already.

"He's in the hospital," Nella said. "You don't need to go tonight. They'll take care of him. Come on, Angela. Let someone else take care of him."

"You don't know what a flashback's like. I can't leave him alone."

"He left you alone! He didn't take care of you!"

Angela spun around. She looked at Nella as if she was speaking another language. Babbling gibberish.

"Because he couldn't! He meant to, but he couldn't."

For the second time that night, Nella watched her hurry away into the dark. How would she ever get to the hospital? She'd walk if she had to. Nothing Nella could say would change her mind. Angela's stubborn, infuriating goodness—nothing could touch it.

"Wait!" Nella shut the door and ran to catch up. She grabbed Angela's shoulder. "Stop! You can't go by yourself."

"Yes I can!" She pulled away.

"All right. I know you can. But Angela, you don't have to."

MORE THAN THREE DIMENSIONS
now

The hospital lounge was a deep freeze. Nella, wet hair, wet feet, was a shiver machine. Dad and Angela were still in Mr. DeMarco's room. Dad had to show ID and answer a zillion questions from the armed policeman outside the doorway. The officer was young, and now he flirted with a pretty nurse, making her laugh. The clock in the lounge said two thirty, but it could as easily be the middle of the day instead of the night. Two doctors bustled by, cheerfully chatting in a language she didn't recognize. When Nella looked at the tall, dark windows, she saw a girl with legs that went on forever. The girl's feet disappeared at the edge of the window, like she'd stepped into some other dimension.

The space-time continuum. Nella's bleary brain finally got it. No boundaries, no *up and down* or *beginning and end*. Everything was relative, every thing and being flowed into every other thing and being, and there were way more than three dimensions. Everything, even the things that seemed to stay still, was moving. Wait till she told Clem she finally understood.

Only she couldn't. Clem was now in a galaxy far far away. . . .

Rem and Bell are measuring time. It comes in sparkly, rainbow-colored drops. In fact, it looks a lot like Jolly Ranchers. They measure it into jars and seal the lids. They touch their light sabers and . . .

"Kiddo?"

She struggled to wake up. Her father's hand was on her shoulder. "Dad." Were her eyes open? She wasn't sure.

"Hey. It's so late."

"But not too late?"

"What?"

Nella sat up. She rubbed her eyes. She'd seen her father bone-tired more times than she could count. But this was different. This was deeper-than-bones tired.

Dad told her the doctors were having trouble calming

Mr. DeMarco down, but when he saw Angela, he held out his arms and she ran to him and he began to . . . cry.

Dad coughed. He had to clear his throat three times before he could speak again.

"He's in rough shape. I had no idea how bad. The doctor said they get way too many vets like him. Some come home with injuries you can see, and some are like Tony DeMarco, with all the wounds on the inside."

Down the corridor, the young policeman softly whistled.

"What's going to happen to him, Dad?"

"They'll keep him here awhile. He'll get treatment and assessment and . . ." Dad massaged the side of his face. "He's got some serious charges against him."

"The gun," whispered Nella.

"Gun?"

"Didn't he have a gun?"

"No, thank God."

He sat down and Nella leaned against him. Her father's shoulder was strong and sturdy. Her goose bumps melted away. She remembered how he'd leaned the ladder against Jeptha A. Stone's shoulder, then set the baby bird back safe and sound in its nest.

"Here she comes." Dad was back on his feet.

"Thank you for bringing me, Mr. Sabatini," said Angela. "I'm sorry we woke you up. You should go home now."

"Hey." Dad smiled. "I'm just glad your father's going to be okay. He's one tough guy."

"That's what everybody thinks." Angela blinked in the fluorescent light. "But it's not really true."

Dad coaxed her to sit down, but she stayed standing.

"He wanted to say he was sorry. That's all. He thought if he could talk to the Andrews family, he could make them see it was all his fault."

"What?" Dad gave her a funny look. "Kiddo, you're so tired. Sit down."

"It was Papa's gun. Anthony took it."

Inside Nella's exhausted brain, the pieces slowly moved together. "That's why Anthony wouldn't say where he got it?" she asked, and Angela nodded.

"But why?" Dad looked baffled. "Why would a kid like Anthony want a gun?"

"He didn't want it. He just wanted Papa not to have it." Angela tugged on a lock of hair. "Because of . . . of how he is. Papa couldn't legally buy a gun, but somehow he managed to get it. Anthony was more and more worried about it. He was scared one of these nights Papa might . . . you know. Hurt himself. One of his army buddies did that."

Anthony was trying to protect his father. His father and Angela. Just like always.

"Anthony saw Papa was getting worse, so he took it and

kept it in his car. That was really stupid, but he did. It was there in the car that night. If only he didn't have it! If only he'd dumped it in the river!"

If only. If only.

"When Papa figured that out, he felt like it was all his fault. He doesn't want anyone to blame Anthony. He . . . he loves Anthony. He just told me how much he . . ." Angela's shoulders sagged like they'd carried a huge weight as long as they could bear. She began to cry. "He wanted to talk to the Andrews family. He meant to explain everything and tell them not to blame Anthony. But he drank too much. And now no one will ever believe him."

NONNI, THE SECRET KEEPER
now

N ella woke with the birds. Tiptoeing downstairs, she
turned on the computer and read the news.

Anthony DeMarco, father of Anthony DeMarco Jr.,
charged with the murder of D'Lon Andrews, is a
veteran of two military tours. During the second
deployment, his unit suffered heavy casualties. Military records show he tried to reenlist but was refused
due to an undisclosed disorder. According to sources,
he has been treated for post-traumatic stress disorder. Arrested near the Andrewses' home, DeMarco

is expected to be charged with driving while intoxi-
cated, menacing, and resisting arrest.

Nella found an article about post-traumatic stress. It said that in the last few years, mental health disorders had caused more hospitalizations among U.S. troops than any other medical condition, including battle wounds. It said—

Barbaric shouts of joy interrupted her. They'd discovered Angela. Moments later, they were all tumbling down the stairs. Angela was smiling, the boys were smiling, Mom was smiling. It was a smile landslide, an unstoppable force of nature.

Mom made chocolate chip pancakes, Angela's old favorite. She said that after breakfast, Angela should go get her clothes and whatever else she needed. Angela carefully set her fork down.

"I'm okay. I can just go home."

"Don't be silly! You can't stay by yourself! You'll stay with us as long as you need to." Mom's words made the boys collapse in a heap of boy-joy. She smoothed Angela's hair, her eyes full of tenderness. "I can braid your hair if you want."

Upstairs, Angela told Nella, "I can go. I really can. I'm used to taking care of myself." She looked at the ceiling. "That sounds so pathetic. Anyway, you don't have to worry. I know you and Clem have plans."

"That's okay. Clem's busy today. Probably tomorrow and the next day, too."

"The special second." Angela remembered now. "I'm sorry. I made you miss it."

"Yeah well." Nella drew a breath. "All seconds should be special. They should all matter."

"You sound like Sister Rosa!"

"That reminds me."

Nonni smiled as if an angel had flown into her room.

"Angela!"

It sounded as if she'd had one too many glasses of Chianti. Angela looked alarmed—she had no idea how bad Nonni was and what progress she'd made. Nonni pointed at a chair, and Angela sat down, hands in her lap. Now Nonni frowned.

"An-tony," she said. *"Soccorso."*

Angela slid a look at Nella, who shook her head and shrugged. *Who knows?* Nonni reached under the bed-covers and pulled out her purse, which she must have been hiding from Gypsy thieves. The same purse she'd had forever. The black leather was worn and shredding, but the clasp could still give your finger a vicious pinch. Nonni scanned the room, as if bandits might appear at any moment, then drew out a single key.

"Sell her."

Angela and Nella traded looks. Oh no. Just when she seemed to be getting better. She'd slid back. She was all confused, like Dad warned.

"Sell who?" Nella tried.

Nonni held up the key and in slow, exaggerated motion, as if she was dealing with a three-year-old, mimed opening a lock.

"Sell her!"

"Seller?" Angela tried, and Nonni nodded.

"Hiring," she said, then pushed at her mouth to make it behave. *"Hiding."*

Nella remembered what Dad said: She got all worked up talking nonsense about the basement.

"Cellar! You mean cellar! But Nonni—no one's hiding down there. I've been checking on your house—you don't need to worry. Actually, I met the girl who lives across the street and she's nice! She told me—"

Nonni waved her hand, cutting Nella short. She took her wallet out of the purse. Pinching thumb and finger together, she drew out a dollar bill and handed it to Angela.

As if one dollar would help! Stingy old Nonni. The key she put in Nella's hand.

"Mule-o," she said. "Mule-o gone day."

The aide bustled in—time for physical therapy.

"My goodness." She winked at Nella. "We're talking up a storm today, aren't we?"

As the aide wheeled her out, Nonni yelled over her shoulder, "Go! Mule!"

Nella and Angela stared at each other. Nella fingered the key. *Mule-o gone day?*

The basement of Nonni's house was dark and chill as a dungeon. A single bare bulb dangled from the ceiling. Nonni didn't believe in saving stuff, so there wasn't much down here besides her artificial Christmas tree, an ancient, empty freezer, PopPop's garden tools. Fastened to a heavy, scarred table was the grinder Nonni used for making sausage. Bend down, and you could still get a delicious, licorice-y whiff of fennel seed.

The basement was always off limits. No kids allowed. It felt wrong to be down here.

"I don't see anything with a lock," Angela said.

"It's hiding, remember?"

For the second time in two days, they were searching, searching side by side. Under the freezer, behind the furnace, under the sausage table. Nella climbed a ladder and poked in the rafters. A hideous spider made her yelp. Angela opened boxes marked DECORAZIONI DI NATALE.

Another repulsive spider! Nella scrambled down the stepladder.

"Look." Angela's voice was hushed. "Nella, look."

She held up a metal box the size of a fat dictionary. A small, gleaming padlock secured the hasp.

Nella's heart began to race. As Angela set the box on the sausage table, she pulled out Nonni's key. Yes. It fit. She lifted the lid.

Molto grande. Huge.

"For the love of God!" said Dad.

The whole family stood around the dining room table. Mom had pushed the army men, Legos, Pampers, and pizza crusts aside. In the middle, in neat, rubber-banded rolls, sat more money than any of them had ever seen.

"Nonni's a millionaire!" breathed Bobby.

"Millin hair!" said Vinny, who was in Angela's arms.

"I can't believe it," said Mom. "I helped her take the Christmas tree down. I carried that box of decorations to the basement myself."

"If I know her, she kept moving the money around." Dad shook his head and grinned. "That batty old lady! She must've been saving for years without a word to anyone."

"Wearing the same thirty-year-old sweater and reusing tea bags the whole time," said Mom.

When Dad pulled off one of the rubber bands, it disintegrated in his fingers. The money sighed as it unrolled.

There were fives, tens, twenties, lots of hundreds. Dad counted out loud, and Nella added it up. She probably made some mistakes, but close enough. She set down her pencil.

"Thirty thousand, six hundred and seventy-four dollars."

"Lub a God!" said Vinny.

"This is what she was trying to tell me, only I thought she was talking out of her head." Dad turned to Nella, his brow creased. "How'd you figure it out, kiddo?"

"I don't know. I guess I just . . . just get her."

Dad's nod was thoughtful.

"She should've put it in the bank," Mom said. "What was she thinking?"

"She's never trusted banks," said Dad. "She came over with everything she owned in one cloth bag, and all her money sewn into the hem of her coat. She and PopPop paid cash for everything."

"Why'd she tell us now, all of a sudden?" asked Salvatore.

"That's a good question." Mom patted his gelled, sprayed pompadour. "Maybe being sick made her start thinking."

"Actually," said Nella. "Actually, I think I know why."

They all looked at her.

"She was saving up in case of something. She didn't know what, but she knew there'd be some disaster. And now there is. She wants us to help Angela's family."

Angela almost dropped Vinny. He laughed and patted her cheek. "Oops!" he said.

Dad continued to give Nella that same thoughtful look. "What makes you say that, Bella?"

"She told us."

"Not really," said Angela. "We're not sure what she said."

"I know," said Nella. *I know.* "I understand Nonni. She wants to help your family."

"But why?" said Angela. "Why would she?"

"Nonni's seen a lot," said Mom. She stood behind Dad and put her arms around him. "A lot of hurt. A lot of sorrow."

"But love, too," whispered Nella. "She's seen a lot of *amore.*"

Mom and Dad both looked at her, their eyes brimming with it.

"No cry!" Vinny patted Angela's wet cheek.

"I'll go talk to Nonni." Dad stood up. "I'm sure she'll tell me exactly what she wants us to do."

What the Statue of Jeptha A. Stone Would Say if It Could

The babies are testing their wings.
They will leave me before long.
Forward! That is the way of our cosmos.
The future is irresistible.

THE NEWS, AGAIN
now

After Dad left, Nella and Angela walked over to her house to fetch her things. Great. The TV van was back out front. That same obnoxious reporter hopped out and hurried toward them. The red-haired cameraman, looking weary, plodded at her heels.

"Let's get out of here," said Nella. "She's not on your side."

Too late.

"You're Angela DeMarco, aren't you?" The reporter was wearing the turquoise suit, which was wrinkled, as if she'd been waiting a long time. "How are you feeling today, Angela?"

341

"How do you think she feels?" snapped Nella.

Turquoise Suit drew back. Her eye shadow was glommed up in the creases. Something brown was stuck between her bottom teeth. The red-haired cameraman peeked out from behind his camera to smile at Nella.

"I wasn't talking to you, sweetheart." The reporter moved in on Angela. "Last night your father was arrested outside the home of the man your brother is charged with killing. That's a pretty terrible situation for a little girl to be in. Can you tell us about your daddy and big brother?"

She tried to stick the microphone in Angela's face, but Nella pushed it away. "She doesn't have to talk to you! She has the right to remain silent."

Turquoise Suit's eyes widened. So did the cameraman's smile.

"It's okay, Nella." Angela stepped forward. "I'm tired of being silent. I want to speak." With that, she lifted the microphone right out of the reporter's hand. She looked the camera straight in the eye.

"My father wanted to say how sorry we are. To say . . . say that we'll be sorry for the rest of our lives. I know that doesn't change what happened. I know . . ."

She hesitated then and glanced at Nella. What? her eyes asked. What do I know? Nella could only look back, trying to encourage her.

342

"We can't change what my brother did that night. No matter how much we want to, we can't. But . . ." Angela twisted a lock of hair. She was getting nervous. Probably she'd just remembered she was saying this in front of thousands of people. She drew a breath. "But maybe, I'm not sure, but maybe what happened can change us. I mean, doesn't it have to? Because otherwise . . ."

All at once she gulped and pushed the microphone into Nella's hand. She was trusting Nella, like so many times before.

"Otherwise," Nella heard herself say. "Otherwise . . . we'll just be sorry, and what's the good of that? That won't make things better." Her voice, that voice from deep inside, grew stronger, like the singing at the vigil, rising, pushing against the darkness. "But maybe if the past shows us what we never, ever want to happen again, maybe it's not really the past anymore. Maybe . . ."

"Maybe," Angela finished, "maybe the past turns into the future."

The reporter stared. She was, possibly for the first time in her life, speechless.

"Amen," breathed the red-haired cameraman.

They all watched the evening news. All except Dad, who still hadn't come back from visiting Nonni.

"There's you!" shouted Sal.

"Angela!" crowed Vinny. "Nella!"

They stood side by side, Angela the angel and Nella the skyscraper. The caption running beneath said, *Angela DeMarco and friend*.

Nella pushed away the microphone, defending Angela. "She has the right to remain silent."

"Good for you!" cried Mom.

Angela said how sorry they were. And then she handed the microphone to Nella. Time didn't stop, or even slow, but Nella saw something she missed in real time, while this was actually happening. Something leaped, shining and sparking, through the air, connecting her and Angela.

"We're going to be sorry all the rest of our lives."

"But maybe if the past shows us what we never, ever want to happen again . . ."

"Maybe the past turns into the future."

The camera zoomed in on the two of them, standing side by side. Their faces filled the screen.

Back to the newsroom.

"Two remarkable little girls," said the news anchor.

Turquoise Suit flashed a smile that might possibly have been genuine. "You can say that again, Jim."

They were still awake when Dad poked his head in Nella's bedroom door.

"Dad! What took you so long?"

He peeked at Vinny, asleep in his youth bed, then stepped across the two of them lying on the floor in their sleeping bags.

"You ever have a day that lasts half a lifetime? While other days go by"—he snapped his fingers—"before you can blink. Last time I checked, the definition of a day was twenty-four hours. So what's the deal?"

"Everything is relative," said Nella.

"What's that even mean?" He sank onto Nella's bed and leaned back on his hands. "It's always sounded fishy to me."

"Dad, just tell us where you were so long!"

"All right." He sat forward, hands on knees, the hallway light falling across his face. "First I went to see Nonni. Before I could say a word, she asked if you'd found the money. You were right, Nella. She wants to help you and your family, Angela."

"But . . ." Angela couldn't believe it. "It's so much money! Doesn't Nonni need it? Or your family?"

"Angela, have you ever tried to argue with that old lady? You might as well argue with a . . . a bird. First we'll post bail. Tomorrow I'll go down to the courthouse and find out what we have to do."

Angela hugged her pillow so tight, why didn't it explode?

"I have to take back every rotten thing I ever said about Nonni," said Nella. "It's going to take me at least five years."

"Next I went to the hospital. He's better today, kiddo. And when he heard the news about Anthony making bail . . ." Dad did some serious throat clearing. "Then something really crazy happened. The cop on duty came in to tell us the Andrews family decided not to press the menacing charges."

"Really? Why?"

"That's what I wanted to know." Dad leaned back on his hands, and his face disappeared into the shadows. His voice floated on the darkness. "So I drove down to the Andrews house."

Despite the heat, Nella pulled the sleeping bag up to her chin. What was her father thinking? They'd never talk to him. He was from Anthony's neighborhood. On Anthony's side. She cringed, thinking of what they must have said to him. Poor Dad!

"All the lights were on, but still it was late to be knocking on someone's door. I just stood there on the lawn, knowing I should turn around. Why would they ever talk to me? If I was them, would I ever trust anybody again?"

Nella pictured the Andrews house the way it looked on the news: crooked awning, toys on the lawn. Wait, no—the toys were on the Manzinis' lawn. And then, who knows why, she saw Marie, reaching for something invisible.

"While I was standing there trying to decide what to do, the door opened. It was his fiancée. I was ready for her to slam that door in my face, but instead she listened to me. I started explaining about your father, Angela, and she already knew. Her brother's a veteran, she said. And her uncle. And her cousin, he lost a leg. She knows, she said. She's seen close up."

"I wish I could meet her," whispered Angela.

"I said how sorry we were."

Dad paused again. *Sorry, so sorry.* Those were the words he'd always wanted to say to Marie's family, only they never let him. The words had lodged inside him all these years, unspoken, unheard. A song he never got to sing.

"I started to leave then, but she came outside. Not *she.* Maya, that's her name. Maya said D'Lon always expected the best from people. He told their boys every day, Bad has a big mouth, that's why it gets all the attention. But don't be fooled, he told them. Good doesn't need to brag. Good knows it's stronger." Dad leaned forward, his face emerging from the shadows. "Then Maya said to tell Anthony's sister and her friend she got their message. What did she mean? What was she—"

"Mr. Sabatini?" Angela interrupted. "Do you think . . .

I know it's not up to me, but can we share Nonni's money with Maya's family?"

Dad grew quiet. Nella knew he was thinking the same thing she was: Nonni's love would never stretch that far. She was too old, too set in her ways to help *those* people.

But maybe Dad had also started believing in changing the past.

"We can ask her, Angela."

"Anthony would want us to do it. I know he would."

"We'll see what she says."

Dad lay back on Nella's bed. Within moments, he was out, breathing softly and steadily. She got up and pulled a sheet over him. After a long time, she fell asleep too.

When she woke the next day, her father was still there. He looked so peaceful, like a man forgiven. Like this was the best sleep he'd had in years.

CRAPP

now

NELLA: Hello?

SAM: Do you want to come to my soccer practice tomorrow?

NELLA: You're on a soccer team?

SAM: I'm trying out for the Garfield team. I already met some guys, and all they seemed to care about is how good I am. At soccer, I mean. You should come. It's going to be your school too. Our school.

NELLA: *(trying to sound unexcited)* Okay.

SAM: *(sounding excited)* Great! Wait! There's something I'm supposed to tell you. Clem says—

NELLA: You talked to Clem?

SAM: That is one bizarre girl. She was trying to get this plastic bag out of a tree, only she couldn't reach. She was doing these crazy leaps, like a spazzy ballerina. So I get it for her, and she says, Tell Nella there's a new crap member. I help her and she disses me!

NELLA: Not crap. CRAPP.

SAM: Like I said. Bizarre.

FRIENDSHIP, FATE, AND OTHER COSMIC THINGS
now

Approximately one hundred eighty seconds after the phone call, Clem's father, complete with bow tie, opened the door.

"Our own Little Nell! Come in."

"I just wanted to give this to Clem." She held out Nonni's grabber claw. Dr. Patchett feigned terror. *Feigned* was a word that didn't work for everyone, but it fit Clem's father perfectly.

"Hold your weapon!" he cried. "I surrender!"

"Patch!" Clem appeared at the edge of the room. "Don't be so ridiculous."

"Ah, my darling Clementine." He feigned relief. "You take over. I'm too old and feeble for battle!"

Nella held out Nonni's claw. "I heard you were on patrol."

Clem didn't move from the other side of the room. It was a big room, and right now it was bigger than ever before.

"Sam," Clem said. "He's so bizarre."

"He can't help it. He's a boy."

Clem let a smile slip out. She pushed her heavy glasses up her nose. Nella continued to hold out the claw. Her arm was starting to get tired.

"Did you . . . did you still take the picture?"

Clem pulled her bandanna lower on her forehead and nodded. "Do you want to see it?"

"Okay."

Nella followed her into her room. Her wonderful room. She set the claw down, and Clem handed her the phone. Nella nearly dropped it.

"*That's* where you took the picture?" Nella couldn't believe it. Clem stood in front of Nella's house!

"I still wanted you to be part of it."

"I wanted to be, too."

Clem carefully lifted the top off Mr. T's house.

"I saw you both on TV. I didn't get it before. I never

knew anybody like her, with a family like that, and problems like that." Clem lowered her hand and let Mr. T sniff her fingers. "I guess it just didn't compute."

"It's not your fault." Nella came to stand next to her.

"Yes it is. When you're always focused on the big cosmic picture, you can miss the earthly details." She pressed a finger to her temple. "It was like *ow. Ow ow.* Like my brain was made of stone and it got a big crack in it."

Mr. T squeaked.

"I'm not saying the Leap Second wasn't monumental. It was! But there'll be another one in a couple of years. That's the thing with time. It keeps happening." Clem lifted the hedgehog out and spoke to him. "You should've seen her! She zoomed across the playground like a superhero defying the dark forces of evil."

"Don't believe her," Nella told the hedgehog. "She's really, really nearsighted. She probably needs new glasses again."

GAD, Clem put the hedgehog in Nella's hands. When he squeaked, the soft under-part of him thrummed. Nella needed to tell Clem how confusing everything still was. How many crucial things she still didn't understand, like friendship, and goodness, and courage. Not to mention God and fate and boys and other cosmic things. Maybe she'd never understand, or maybe there weren't the right words, or maybe she just didn't know them yet. Maybe she was still figuring out how to talk.

"Vinny can talk now," she told Clem. "One day he said *Angela*. And he hasn't shut up since."

"That's called a chain reaction. That's this thing in chemistry where the products of one reaction contribute directly to a further reaction. For example, a bombardment of neutrons."

"I thought you'd never speak to me again."

Clem picked up the claw and pinched her. "Do you want some pomegranate juice? It's the new papaya."

While she was gone, Nella held fast to Mr. T. It was difficult to feel a hedgie's heart, surrounded by all that armor, but she thought she could.

NOW AND ALWAYS

Angela and Anthony visited their father every day. He'd been transferred to a rehab center. Angela said she hated the place, and Nella said tell me about it.

When Maya got the money they sent her, she sent them something back. A photo of the two boys. The big one, D'Lon Jr., smiled nicely. The little one, Cassius, made a face.

Bobby always ruined family photos the same way.

Anthony kept it in his wallet, Angela said. Someday he hoped he'd get to meet them.

"He'll go to jail," Angela said. "We know that. I just

hope it's not too far away."

"My dad will take you to see him," Nella promised. "No matter how far it is, I know he will."

They were sitting on Nella's front porch, the cemetery wall looming across the street. Some vine Dad planted spilled over the top, all starry with white flowers. The two of them were quiet, till Angela unexpectedly laughed.

"I almost forgot! Guess who I saw at Papa's rehab?"

"Sister Rosa."

"I couldn't believe it. She had on hot-pink Crocs with sparkle stickers, and she was in the art room helping these guys twice as big as she is mix up paints. They love her! She was just the same, only more. She made me feel like . . . like I don't know. Like you should never give up. Because you never know when goodness is going to come showering down."

The starry flowers stirred in the soft breeze. Vinny came out and sat in between them.

"You know what else she did?" Angela said then. "She got some kind of divine statue museum to take St. A. She said he'll probably find life there too quiet and boring after the playground, so she'll take us on a field trip to visit him. Want to come, Vin?"

"Me come."

"I promised Sister I'd tell you hello. So. Hello, Nella."

"Hello, Angela."

That evening, just before supper, Nella walked up the hill. Past Franny's, past the window with T-shirts saying THE BEST PEOPLE HAVE A ROOT IN THE BOOT, past Mama Gemma's where "I did it my way!" ran on its torturous loop, past Nonni's corner and Clem's corner and a sidewalk tree whose leaves had a tinge of autumn red. The street was clogged with rush-hour traffic, people trying to get up or down the hill, everyone wanting to get home.

As Nella's long legs carried her higher and higher, she trailed a hand along the thick stone wall her long-ago relatives built. A yellow-flecked bird, so small it hardly seemed real, perched on the wall and tried out its voice. Wait. Nella stood still. Could it be?

"Is everything okay?" Nella looked up to see her father coming toward her on the sidewalk. He looked worried. Worried—it was Dad's default setting.

He didn't remember how she used to come meet him, so she could have him all to herself for a little while before she had to share him with the brutish barbarians. How much she'd loved those walks, her hand in his. But that was all right. She smiled to let him know everything was all right.

"Hey. Know what I was thinking about just now? How you used to meet me here on the hill. You were always asking me questions. Know what you asked me once?"

"Something dumb, no doubt."

"How come the sky's so high up? Why didn't God put it lower, so you could pat the clouds?"

"I told you!"

They fell into step together, and then Dad said, "Maybe that's why you were drawn to that other Marie. The statue is like you."

"What?" Nella was horrified. "I'm not dead!"

"The way she's reaching, I mean."

"But it's sad. She'll never get what she wants. It's always too far away."

"Oh, she's going to get it, don't worry, kiddo. Even if it's the moon and the stars, someday that girl's going to get it."

Dad caught Nella's hands and swung them high over her head. For a moment they stood there, fingertip to fingertip, reaching for the wide-open sky.

A Final Word
from the
Honorable Jeptha A. Stone

I, Jeptha A. Stone, was never a fan of surprises.

They are, as I am certain you agree, undignified.

Yet even after death, that scalawag called Life continues to play its tricks.

While these baby birds test their wings, while they perch upon my broad shoulders and my handsome aquiline nose, I am surprised and grateful to learn:

Nothing ever truly ends.

Something new forever begins.

Goodness sings its song.

Time spins its golden circle.

Dignity is overrated.

Hark unto me, Jeptha . . . Oh never mind.

I have the feeling you already know.

You know.